The Stepsisters

#6 Guilty Sister

Tina Oaks

SCHOLASTIC INC.
New York Toronto London Auckland Sydney

ISBN 0-590-41464-X

12 11 10 9 8 7 6 5 4 3 2 1   8 9/8 0 1 2 3/9

Printed in the U.S.A.   01

First Scholastic printing, June 1988

Guilty Sister

The Stepsisters

CHAPTER 1

One bright fall morning, Virginia Mae Guthrie Whitman called a family meeting in the living room of the yellow Victorian house situated at the top of a Philadelphia hill. The family responded obediently, with just a trace of nervousness among the children. There was always the chance that one or more of the four girls and one boy, living together since Virginia Mae's marriage to lawyer William Whitman, had bent or broken a family rule. Racking their brains to remember any such offense, the five silently took their seats in the warm, cozy living room, eyes on their parents, now sitting side by side on a cream-colored loveseat. Five pairs of eyes noted that Virginia Mae was smiling. Elegant as always in the beige suit she wore that day for her duties as a museum guide, her hands were folded easily in her lap, and there were no tension lines in her lovely face. Virginia Mae was not at all dif-

1

ficult to get along with, and they all knew that. But broken rules made her unhappy.

Seeing her stepmother's smile, Paige Whitman, at sixteen the oldest of the four girls, relaxed on the sofa. She let long legs slide out in front of her and clasped her arms behind her head, where her long, silky dark hair had been caught up in a ponytail. Fifteen-year-old Katie Summer Guthrie, her slim sturdy athlete's body wrapped in a pink sweatsuit, sat at attention between her ten-year-old sister, Mary Emily, and Paige. Katie's blonde hair contrasted sharply with Paige's dark hair and eyes, while red-haired Megan, Paige's ten-year-old sister and Mary Emily's new best friend, provided even more of a contrast.

"Tuck," Virginia Mae called as her seventeen-year-old son came into the room, "why don't you take that rocking chair?" Her soft southern drawl warmed all of them. An Atlanta, Georgia, journalist before her marriage, these few months in Pennsylvania had done nothing to change her natural speech patterns. It always amazed Paige that although she found Katie's accent maddeningly irritating, she found exactly the same sounds coming from her stepmother's mouth charming. But then, so *many* things about Katie Summer Guthrie irritated her.

"We've decided," Virginia Mae announced, "that it's time to buy another car."

Paige whooped with delight. Katie Summer clapped her hands together, while the younger girls wondered, wide-eyed, what a new car would mean to them. And a usually uninterested Tuck sat up straighter in the rocking chair. "What kind of car?" he wanted to know. "Not another station wagon?"

Virginia Mae shook her head. "No, something smaller. One of the medium-sized sedans, we thought," she said, glancing over at her husband. "Easier to drive in city traffic."

Tuck looked disappointed. "American cars are boring." He was thinking that a snazzy red sports car would be much more likely to impress people. And he certainly hadn't had much luck impressing people in this northern city so far. He especially wanted to impress one beautiful, popular girl at school named Jennifer Bailey. The guy she was dating, Ed Thomas, drove a red sports car.

His mother smiled. "Maybe they are boring," she said, "but they seem safer."

"And repairs are cheaper," her husband added.

Watching them, Paige thought, not for the first time, what a handsome couple they made. Her father's dark good looks went well with Virginia Mae's southern fairness. And he always looked so relaxed when Virginia Mae's hand was in his. The lines that eight years of being a widower raising two daughters had etched across his face had all but disappeared. The marriage, with its combined families, had so far been like a roller-coaster ride: up one minute, down the next. But through it all, her father had kept that special look that was in his eyes when he looked at his new wife. Paige liked that look. It made her feel . . . safe. Like they'd always be a family now, no matter what. In spite of the fact that she and Virginia Mae's blonde, beautiful daughter Katie

Summer had so far mixed like oil and water. In spite of the fact that Tuck was about as pleased with moving to Philadelphia as she, Paige, would have been with moving to Atlanta, which was not at *all*. In spite of differences and disagreements and disillusionments, her father still looked at Virginia Mae like that. So it was okay.

And now they were getting a new car! And good old Katie Summer didn't even have a driver's license yet, so the new car was the *one* thing she wouldn't have to share with Ms. Scarlett Unbearable. Bad enough she had to share a not-so-large bedroom with the Belle of Atlanta, who actually *collected* perfume samples and nested them in a ruffled basket on the dresser in their room. At least she wouldn't have to argue over the use of the new car the way they argued over who was getting the bathroom first. Maybe there *was* justice in the world, after all.

This notion was quickly dispelled by Virginia Mae's next remark. "It's time for Katie Summer to apply for her learner's permit."

Paige groaned silently and slumped down in her seat. Her father, seeing the pained expression on her face, sent her a warning glance. Don't start anything, his eyes, dark like hers, said.

"And," Virginia Mae continued, blissfully unaware of Paige's annoyance, "two cars in a family with three active teenagers and two busy parents doesn't seem to be sufficient, as ridiculous as that seems. Paige stays late at school for her work on the newspaper, Katie has swim team, and," smiling at Tuck, "Tuck will be needing a car for dates

4

and a busy social life." She didn't add "any day now," but a flushed and scowling Tuck heard it in her voice. She might just as well have said it aloud as far as he was concerned. Everyone in this newly combined family knew his social life stank. When he did go out, he often went alone. At school he found his drawl mocked by other boys and his southern manners the subject of countless jokes. And the only girl who appealed to him, Jennifer Bailey, was already semi-attached to a football bruiser who gave new meaning to the expression, "All brawn and no brains."

So what did *he* need a new car for? Let Katie Summer and Paige fight over it the way they fought over everything else.

Katie began chattering with her usual enthusiasm about the type and color of the proposed car.

Her stepfather stopped her. "Whoa, there!" he called, waving one hand in the air. "Before you get carried away, we need to establish a few ground rules."

At the word rules, Katie and Paige emitted low groans. Tuck looked suspicious.

"First of all," Bill Whitman elaborated, "there will be *no* fighting over the use of this new vehicle. If you're adult enough to drive, you're adult enough to share responsibly Your mother and I don't intend to get involved in any hassles about the use of this car. Got that?"

They all nodded with a singular lack of enthusiasm.

"Secondly," Bill continued, "when all three of you older children are licensed drivers, I expect

5

you to relieve your mother of many of her errands and her chauffeuring duties involving the two younger children."

Megan and Mary Emily beamed. Paige, Katie, and Tuck did not.

"And last, but certainly not least," their father concluded, looking directly at Paige, "I expect that Katie will have no trouble finding experienced drivers to help her get her license. Your mother and I will help, too, of course. But we won't always be available when she wants to get road practice. That's where you and Tuck come in, Paige."

The thought of being stuck in a car with her stepsister while one was actually trying to *teach* the other something made the hairs on the back of Paige's neck stand at attention. They could barely carry on a decent conversation without arguing. How on earth could her father expect her to be Katie's *teacher*, even for a little while? She wondered resentfully if her stepmother would be suggesting the new car if Katie wasn't about to get her license.

Oh, well, never mind. It would be a while before Katie actually got to drive the car solo.

It would be great to have a car to drive during the week, especially with cold weather coming on before too long.

But teaching Katie to drive? Even if she had the time, which she certainly didn't, there were at least a million other things she'd rather do than be imprisoned in a car with Katie Summer. Like enlisting in the army, or dancing on hot coals, or climbing the Empire State Building . . . on the *outside*. "They'll teach Katie to drive in Driver's Ed," Paige pointed out, hope in her voice.

"Yes," Bill agreed, "but she'll need plenty of practice in the car she'll be driving when she takes her road test."

Paige let out a small sigh.

A look of alarm spread across Katie's face. She had no objection to driving lessons from her mother, her stepfather, or her brother. But from Paige? Just the two of them? In the car? Where do you *go* when you're in a car with someone who makes you crazy? Katie stifled a giggle. When you stop to think about it, she thought to herself, maybe Paige *should* be the one to give driving lessons, since she was such an expert at driving . . . people crazy.

The giggle vanished quickly. She'll call me stupid, an unhappy little voice inside Katie's head moaned. She'll call me stupid and say, "Why don't you know anything useful?" And when she's not doing that, she'll be bossing me around as if I were a child. I can't *stand* the thought!

"Now," Bill said, "are we all clear on what this new car will mean to everyone?"

Katie, who couldn't stand the thought of what it meant, nodded dutifully. And Paige, who was trying to convince herself that there was no way Katie would ever pass a road test, nodded, too.

"Well," Virginia Mae said briskly, standing up, "that's settled then. Now all we have to do is find a little car that will be suitable."

Paige rolled her eyes at Tuck. If Virginia Mae

was going to seek out a "suitable" car, it would probably be a dark-colored sedan that went no faster than twenty miles an hour. Paige entertained a momentary vision of herself tooling around town in a sleek foreign red sports car, its top down, her long black hair blowing free in the wind. That image disappeared quickly with one glance at Virginia Mae's calm, no-nonsense expression. The car, Paige reminded herself sternly, would be "sensible." Oh, well, no point in being picky. Wheels, after all, were wheels.

The car they selected was indeed, at least from the point of view of the three teenagers, "sensible." It was a medium-sized Chevrolet sedan, maroon in color. It brought a satisfied smile to Virginia Mae's face, and a sigh of resignation from her three older children. It was an attractive car with a pleasant "brand-new" smell to it, its upholstery a luxurious cream color. Megan and Mary Emily pronounced it, "Neat!" Paige complained mildly that blue was a much nicer color than maroon, Katie nervously wondered aloud if it wasn't a little big, and Tuck lounged against the car looking bored.

"It has automatic transmission," Virginia Mae pointed out cheerfully. "I didn't want you kids wrestling with a clutch."

Tuck yawned. A sports car would have had a clutch. And learning to use one wouldn't have killed them. He shrugged and walked away wondering just how long it would be before Paige and Katie were at each other's throats over the new car.

The truth was, although Tuck made a show of being unconcerned, he hated the fighting that went on in the Whitman-Guthrie household. They'd never fought much back in Atlanta. Minor disagreements over who was supposed to do which chore, or who had left the light on in the bathroom when their mother was struggling to keep utility bills to a minimum, or which person needed a new winter jacket the most, things like that. Never anything really serious, not really. Virginia Mae thought fighting among siblings was "distasteful." How she must hate what was going on now! If she didn't love Bill so much. . . .

It always came back to that, for Tuck. He hated Philadelphia, he didn't like this new combined family particularly, and he was *not* having the good time his mother had promised him when they'd first discussed this major move. But in spite of the "distasteful" fighting among the siblings, despite the tension in the house, Tuck knew his mother was happy. And that was something, after all the years she'd been alone. They'd had a good life in Atlanta, but even with all the friends his mother had, he'd known there was something missing in her life. Now she'd found it, and he was glad for her.

Besides, he was nearly finished with high school. Then he could take off, go wherever he wanted, leave the two squabbling sisters behind him forever.

Which was why he didn't get too excited when Bill started mentioning college, and especially when he mentioned the possibility of Tuck attending college "in the area." "We're just getting to know you," he'd said genially one evening recently. "Hate to think of you going off somewhere so soon. Lots of good schools right around here, Tuck, Hope you'll pick one of those."

Not likely. Not likely at all, Tuck thought. It was back south for him.

CHAPTER 2

Probably because Paige shared Tuck's premonition about civil war breaking out, she managed to avoid driving instructor duty with Katie during the first week after the new car arrived. Virginia Mae, Tuck, and Bill filled the teacher's slot at first. Paige used as excuses her schoolwork, which in her junior year was considerable, her work on the school newspaper, which was important, and her relationship with Ben Collins, coeditor of the paper. This was the same Ben who, when she told him about the new car and her promise to help teach Katie how to drive, threw his head backward and laughed heartily, startling everyone in the newsroom. It wasn't like Ben to be that expressive. Normally, he was reserved, seldom giving away his emotions. Trying to guess what Ben was feeling was a challenge that kept Paige busy.

She stared at him, open-mouthed at his reaction to her announcement that she intended to teach Katie to drive.

After a moment, he removed his glasses and wiped his eyes. *"You?"* he asked hoarsely. "You're going to teach Katie Summer how to drive?" His thin face split with a wide grin. "C'mon, Paige, get real! You and Katie Summer can't even be in the same room without sending off sparks. And you expect to sit alone in a car with her?" His grin got wider. "You just can't pass up the chance to give her orders, can you?"

"This is *not* my choice, Ben. It's part of the deal — if I don't help with the driving lessons, I don't get a crack at the new car." She was strangely annoyed by his implication that she couldn't get along with her stepsister. Never mind that Ben in particular had good reason to make the implication, since Paige regularly complained to Ben about Katie. But she had been hoping that he had noticed how hard she'd been trying to keep peace with Katie Summer. Apparently he hadn't. That was disappointing. What was the point in being a wonderfully patient, tolerant, adult-type sister if one of the most important people in your life didn't even notice?

"I can teach her," she said haughtily as Ben returned to the copy he was editing. She loved the intense way he had of peering down, examining each word carefully, as if he had it under a microscope. Ben took his duties as coeditor as seriously as he took everything else in life. (Except, maybe, *her* relationship with her new family. He didn't take that half as seriously as she did.)

Laurie, Ben's coeditor, came over to hand him a sheaf of papers. "Urgent!" she said, Then she went back to her seat. Ben held the papers and focused his hazel eyes on Paige. "Sure, you could teach her," he said calmly. "If you wanted to. But you don't. What you really want is for her to get into that new car, drive all the way to Georgia where she came from, and *stay* there. Am I right or am I right?"

Paige grinned. "Well," she said lightly, "she can't do that until she gets her license, can she? That's motivation enough to help her get it, right?"

Shaking his head, Ben read Laurie's papers. Reluctantly, Paige left his side and went to her own desk. She was used to the clatter of busy typewriters, so they failed to interfere with her thinking processes. If only Ben could understand what it was like for her, living with a stepsister! If she and Katie were more alike, having a new sister her own age might have been fun. Mary Emily Guthrie was a doll, but she was only ten years old. Seeing the way Megan and Mary Emily had become instantly attached often made Paige envious. Why couldn't Katie and Paige have developed an instant friendship? But Paige had absolutely nothing in common with the trim and neat Ms. Guthrie from Atlanta.

"She's cotton candy," Judy Belnap, Paige's best friend, had once pointed out, "and you're pickles. But," she had pointed out quickly, "a lot of people *like* pickles."

Well, maybe. But not as much as they liked cotton candy. Not as much as they liked pretty, popular Katie Summer Guthrie, with her soft, flirty southern drawl, and her impressive performance on the swim team, and the way she looked

13

in, of all things, a sweat suit. She is, Paige thought with a sense of defeat, the only person in the world who can make a fashion statement wearing sweats!

Why couldn't Ben see how hard Katie's arrival on the scene had been for Paige? Then maybe he'd understand why she wanted Katie Summer to get in the new car, drive to Atlanta, Georgia, and stay there.

When Bill Whitman realized Paige hadn't been spending any time with Katie in the new car as she'd promised, he put his foot down, ordering her to keep her promise. She didn't argue. She'd run out of excuses, anyway. Her father handed her the keys to the car while Katie stood in the foyer, shifting from one foot to the other nervously.

"Thanks," Paige told her father. Turning to Katie, she asked brusquely, "Well? Shall we get this over with?"

The driving lesson was a disaster from start to finish. Katie, nervous at being alone with Paige, couldn't seem to do anything right. Her lessons with other members of the family had gone well, and she'd begun feeling a bit more self-confident behind the wheel of the new Chevy. But that self-confidence vanished in the face of Paige's impatient sighs. Katie stalled the car twice before the engine caught. Then she gave it too much gas, and the car lurched violently backward as she moved the automatic gearshift into reverse. That brought a startled gasp from Paige. The sound rattled Katie's nerves further. She backed down the long, steep driveway, steering so erratically that Paige cried, "Katie, *slow down* and watch where you're going! You almost took out a chunk of the stone wall. On *my* side!"

They screeched out of the driveway and came to a jarring halt in the street. "I'm sorry," Katie apologized in a shaky voice. "I guess I'm a little nervous."

"Then you shouldn't be behind the wheel of a car," Paige said primly. "Not one with *me* in it, anyway. Maybe I'd better drive."

"No," Katie said in a firm voice. "*I* will drive. I'm okay now." Taking a deep breath, she stiffened her shoulders and clamped both hands on the steering wheel. "Let's get this show on the road. I have a date tonight."

Paige didn't ask who was taking Katie out that night. She knew it was Jake Carson, the very same future law student and present Whitman family handyman in whom Paige had once pinned her own romantic hopes. Until Katie came along.

Katie had spoken too soon when she said, "I'm okay now." She wasn't. Determination alone couldn't make up for her lack of experience. And tension so thick it coated the front seat like a slipcover stole away the little bit of self-confidence she had accumulated in earlier lessons.

She oversteered and ran her back wheels over the curb. The bump startled both driver and instructor.

"Will you *please* watch where you're going?"

"Sorry." And how many times, an embarrassed Katie wondered, am I going to mumble *that* phrase on this beautiful Saturday afternoon?

"Just watch where you're going, okay?"

15

At the next intersection, Katie stalled the car again. Although she quickly got it started, several people behind her in the busy Saturday afternoon traffic honked impatiently as the light changed from red to green.

"Honestly, Katie, you'd think this was the first time you'd ever been behind the wheel of a car!"

The words echoed in Katie's frazzled brain: "Honestly, Katie, honestly, Katie, honestly, Katie. . . ." She wanted to scream, Honestly, Paige, you're supposed to be teaching me, not shouting at me! But she didn't. The hour of instruction stretched ahead of her like a poisonous snake. Screaming at Paige wasn't going to help her get through it. It would just make matters worse — if such a thing were possible.

Paige said, "Take a right at the next corner."

Katie promptly flipped on the left-hand turn signal.

"Don't you know your left from your right?"

Katie made the correction, while she tried to figure out how she could (*a*) crash the car so that the impact hit only on Paige's side and (*b*) how to make it look like an accident. Deciding she had her hands full just trying to *drive* the stupid car, never mind maneuvering it in any particular way, she bit her lower lip and concentrated on concentrating.

But it was hopeless. Street signs blurred, divider lines in the road faded, and she lost any sense of which was right and which left. After nearly being sideswiped by a tractor-trailer impatient with her turtle's pace, she pulled over to the curb and switched off the ignition, willing her legs to stop shaking. She sat behind the wheel, clenching her hands.

"As a driver," Paige said after a moment, her voice full of disgust, "you're a great swimmer."

"And as a teacher," Katie snapped back, "you're a royal pain in the neck! *You* drive," she ordered as she opened the car door and jumped out. "Let me see how an expert does it!"

Ignoring the sarcasm in her sister's voice, Paige nodded. "Good idea."

As angry at Katie was, she had to admit as they drove home that Paige handled the car pretty well. Well, of course she does, she told herself. She's had her license for months now. You shouldn't compare yourself to her. You know better than that.

But sometimes she did it, anyway, in spite of an earlier resolution not to. After all, they were two entirely different human beings. But some-things were harder to ignore than others: like Paige and Virginia Mae's common interest in writing, a bond that Katie had never shared with her mother. She was aware of the disappointment that had registered on her mother's face as she'd watched Katie struggle with every written sentence in a number of assigned compositions over the years. And Paige and Virginia Mae both played the piano, while Katie couldn't have carried a tune in a suitcase. She wasn't used to shar-ing her mother with someone, except for Mary Emily and Tuck, of course, and that was differ-ent. She *liked* Tuck and Mary Emily; *that* was the difference.

It was different, too, sharing her mother with

Bill. That didn't sting at all. It was so neat to see her mother happy and in love again for the first time since Katie's father had, as she put it, "taken a hike." And it was great having a handsome, smart, warm, and funny stepfather. She understood how her mother felt about Bill, and she unstood why.

But she would never understand Paige Elizabeth Whitman if they shared the same bedroom for a thousand years. Katie shuddered at the thought, picturing the horrible mountain of mess that Paige's half of the bedroom could accumulate in that length of time. It took less than one full weekend for Paige's bed to completely disappear under a pile of soiled clothing, wet towels, opened books and magazines, empty bags once filled with junk food, and an assortment of other items Paige collected during her weekend and didn't feel like putting away in their proper places.

So calm, so cool, so collected, Katie thought, glancing over at her stepsister, so confident behind the wheel. Who would think to look at her that she was a grade-A, number-one, blue-ribbon slob? She always looked so neat, so pulled together . . . ha! If people only knew.

Because neither could think of anything pleasant to say to the other, they rode all the way home in an icy silence.

CHAPTER 3

When Katie Summer stormed into the house, followed closely by a grim Paige, Tuck was stretched out on the living room sofa, reading. Seeing the expression on his sister's face, he said, "Oh-oh. The lesson didn't go too well, I take it?"

"Never again!" Paige declared before Katie could say a word. She thrust her jacket at the coat rack in the hall. "Certain people are just too dense to learn something new!"

"And certain people," Katie shot back, her face red with anger, "are too rude and bossy to be teachers!" Turning to Tuck, she asked, "Where's Mom?"

"She took Megan and Mary Emily shopping. Personally," he added lazily, "I think it was just a ploy to get out of the house. She didn't want to be here when you two returned from your exercise in futility. Good thinking on her part, if you ask me."

19

"Well, I *didn't* ask you." Katie was disappointed that her mother wasn't home to provide a dose of much-needed sympathy. "So kindly keep your opinions to yourself."

Tuck shrugged and returned to his book, muttering, "You *asked*." He glanced at Paige. "She asked me where Mom was, and I told her, right?"

Close to tears, Katie whirled and ran up the stairs. But where could she go to get the privacy she needed? Paige was probably right behind her. The thing about sharing a room was that you never felt private even when the room was empty. Even when Paige was absent, there was her messy half of the room staring back at Katie as if to say, "See? You don't have a place of your own anymore."

And if she escaped into the bathroom, in five minutes or less Paige would be hammering on the door, shouting, "How long are you going to hibernate in there? There *are* other people in this house, you know!"

Yes, I *know*, Katie thought as she locked the bathroom door and moved to the little window beside the sink. I *know* there are other people in this house. And one of them is rude and bossy and selfish!

She stood at the window, listening for the sound of Paige's footsteps on the stairs.

But Paige had no intention of following Katie upstairs. She had gone straight to the kitchen to call her best friend. Sitting on a high stool beside the yellow flowered wall, she dialed Judy Belnap's number.

"You wouldn't believe it," she concluded her

story a few moments later. "*Megan* could drive better than Katie Summer Guthrie, and Megan is only ten years old. I can't believe anyone in his right mind would give this girl a driver's license!"

Paige knew she'd made a mistake when Judy made the sound low in her throat that signaled disapproval. Judy liked Katie. But then, who didn't? Paige knew one person who didn't. Well, let the others all try living with Katie Summer twenty-four hours a day. See how *they* would like it!

"Don't you remember," Judy asked, "what it was like when you learned to drive? How hard it was? Remember, it felt like the car was a thousand feet wide and the road only an inch wide?"

"Of course I remember. What's that got to do with anything? At least I listened when my dad told me what to do. When I tell Katie to go left, she turns on her right-hand signal. When I say stop, her foot goes down on the gas pedal. She doesn't listen!"

"That's because you get her all rattled," Judy said calmly. "She knows how you feel about her. And if I know you, Paige, and I *do*, you haven't made any secret of the fact that you despise the idea of teaching your stepsister how to drive. Don't you think that just might make her a little nervous? No wonder she doesn't know left from right."

This was one of those increasingly frequent times when Paige wondered why Judy was still her best friend. In so many of the conflicts between Paige and Katie, Judy seemed to take Katie's side. So why wasn't she *Katie's* best

21

friend? Not that Katie needed any more friends. Paige was the one who couldn't afford to lose a single friend. And because she knew that, she swallowed her anger, saying reluctantly, "Okay, okay. Maybe I was a little rough on her. But sometimes she acts so stupid."

"Only when *you're* around," Judy pointed out. "Maybe it has something to do with her knowing you think she's stupid."

Paige hesitated, then said slowly, "You really think I'm nasty, don't you?"

"No!" Judy spoke with emphasis. "Actually, I think you're pretty terrific. I'm still your best friend, Paige, and I want to stay your best friend. I just think you let your jealousy and your resentment toward Katie Summer get in the way of who you really are."

Paige groaned. "I don't even *know* who I really are anymore."

The unintentional grammatical error made them both laugh, and the conversation ended on a light note.

But after Paige had replaced the receiver, she remained on the stool, lost in thought. Maybe Judy was right. Learning to drive wasn't so easy. Handling a car for the first time could be a really scary thing. And there were so many rules and laws to remember. She had, she remembered, been grateful that her father had been so patient and understanding when he'd taught her to drive.

Sliding from the stool, Paige made a sour face. Being nice to Katie seemed so easy for other people. Why is it so hard for me? she wondered. The answer came, loud and clear: Because you don't want her here.

Grabbing an apple from a fruit basket on the table, Paige left the room, vigorously pushing open the swinging door.

When Katie and Jake returned from a party late that night, Katie tried to explain her feelings to him. "She just makes me feel so stupid! And then I *act* stupid, which just makes her act smug." She shook her head sorrowfully. "Can't say that I blame her. Everybody likes to be right, and Paige is certainly no exception."

"She's *not* right." Jake sat beside Katie on the porch swing, his arm around her shoulders. The autumn air was chilly, but Katie was reluctant to leave the privacy of the porch for the warmth of the house where a member of the family might overhear their conversation. They had both been wise enough to wear heavy sweaters, which did a good job of protecting them from the cool night air. "You'll be a fine driver. You have great coordination, your timing is perfect, thanks to competitive swimming, and you're sensible. You can't miss."

Katie continued to stare at her hands, a frown creasing her forehead.

"Look, if you want," Jake continued earnestly, facing her, "*I'll* take Paige's turn teaching you. Then you won't have to deal with her."

At first, Katie brightened visibly at his offer. Then she shook her head. "Thanks, Jake, that's really sweet of you. But Bill would never allow it.

He has this thing about responsibility. You know that. And Paige promised to help me learn to drive. He'll hold her to that promise even if I don't *want* her help."

Jake nodded. "Yeah, I guess you're right. But any time you feel you need some extra hours behind the wheel, let me know, okay? I'll be glad to take you out on the road." He smiled. "Any excuse to spend more time with you."

Katie returned his smile, her blue eyes shining in the glow of the porch light. Her on-again, off-again romance with Jake Carson was obviously very much "on" at this point. She sighed as Jake pulled her close to his chest. A person just never knew with someone like Jake. He had plans, he said. He was going off to law school, he said. Couldn't get involved, he had told her. As if his going off to law school in the future somehow canceled their feelings for each other *now*. She knew he felt something for her, something good and strong. But so far, every time she relaxed and allowed herself to show her feelings, Jake pulled back. She was almost expecting it again, any day now.

But for now, warm in Jake's arms where she could blot out Paige and driving lessons and feeling stupid, she would just relax and enjoy what she had at his particular moment. She'd deal with Jake's need to cool it when and if it came.

"Did I tell you you look really great tonight?" he asked, his chin resting on her head. "That sweater matches your eyes."

"No, it doesn't," she corrected teasingly. "My

eyes aren't one hundred percent wool and they weren't knit in Switzerland."

Jake laughed and pulled her closer. "The *color*, Katie, the color!"

Their laughter rang in the air, loud enough for Paige, upstairs in her room with the window open a crack, to hear. Her date with Ben had ended early and on an unsatisfactory note. She had made the mistake of opening up to him about her driving lesson with Katie. I should have known better, she reflected, lying in bed staring up at the ceiling. Sometimes Ben listened attentively to her complaints about her family situation . . . and sometimes he didn't. Tonight had been a "didn't" night.

"Oh, give it up, Paige," he'd snapped in the middle of her tirade. "Put a lid on it! Can we please talk about something else tonight? I'm tired of being Katied to death!"

Unfortunately, Paige wasn't able to concentrate on any other subject. After fifteen minutes of a stiff, awkward silence, Ben had brought her home. A quick peck on the cheek had replaced her usual sweet good-night kiss.

And after an evening like that, she thought, burrowing deeper under the covers, I have to lay here and listen to the two of them laughing it up. This has *not* been a good day.

Sunday began in the same vein for Paige. She had barely finished her orange juice when her father summoned her into the living room, where morning sunshine bathed the pastel room in a warm glow. So why, she wondered as she sat down opposite her stern-faced father, do I feel so chilly? Maybe because I know what's coming?

Paige's sense of dread was justified. Because what was coming was a hearty dose of her father's disapproval. "Paige, I'm tired of having these conversations with you about the way you treat your stepsister."

Paige sat up very straight on the sofa, indignation apparent in her body language. "I haven't done anything! And we've been getting along okay."

"Until yesterday," Bill Whitman reminded her, his voice as chilly as Paige felt. "I understand your turn with Katie behind the wheel was unpleasant, to say the least."

Paige squirmed in her seat. That little tattletale! She'd gone running to him, knowing he'd punish Paige.

"It wasn't Katie who told me," he said, reading the expression on her face. "It doesn't matter how I heard about it. The point is, you promised to help your sister learn to drive, and I'm holding you to that promise."

Paige hated it when her father called Katie her "sister." Katie was her *step*sister. And as far as that promise went, it wasn't as if she had made it willingly. She'd had no choice.

"And to help you keep that promise," her father continued, "I've asked Tuck to give up his session with Katie this afternoon and give it to you."

Paige clenched her hands together, trying to

26

stay calm. "But *I* took her out yesterday afternoon," she protested. "That's not fair!"

"*You* will be her instructor this afternoon," Mr. Whitman said firmly, leaving no room for argument. "And I'm telling you right now, Paige, if you repeat yesterday afternoon's performance, it will be a long time before you're allowed access to the new car again. Fair is fair. We had a deal."

Paige couldn't believe he was using the word fair after what he'd just ordered her to do. Another session with Katie? So soon? And she had thought yesterday was a bad day!

"Okay, Dad," she said coldly. It was all she could do to get the words out. "I guess I don't have any choice, do I?"

"Paige. I'm counting on you. If you don't follow through on your promise, I'm going to be very disappointed."

"Right." With as much dignity as she could muster, Paige got up and left the room.

CHAPTER 4

Katie couldn't believe she had to endure another miserable lesson with Paige already. It was Tuck's turn to take her out on the road.

"Dad," she begged her stepfather, "please, it's Tuck's turn! Paige did it yesterday." And the expression on her face gave a clear impression of exactly how well she thought that session had gone.

Bill Whitman was busy rifling through some papers on his desk. But he stopped what he was doing and looked up when she spoke.

"Please," she said simply. "I'll go out on the road with Paige again, this week if you want. But not today, okay? Not so soon?" She hated the note of pleading in her voice, but she couldn't help it. A whole Sunday ruined? I'd rather walk for the rest of my natural life, she thought as she faced Bill Whitman.

"Look, Katie," he said gently, "a bargain is a

bargain. Paige has to learn to follow through on her promises. She promised to help teach you to drive and yesterday afternoon she blew it. If I let her get away with that, she won't learn anything. I'm sorry if it's hard on you."

"It *is!*" she said vehemently, surprising both of them. Immediately sorry, she stammered, "I mean, the lessons are okay with you and Mom and Tuck. But I can't seem to do anything right when Paige is teaching me."

"She'll do better today," her stepfather promised. "I had a little talk with her."

Katie heaved a silent groan. Every time Bill had a "little talk" with Paige, Katie suffered. She'll think I complained to him, she thought in dismay. She probably won't even speak to me. Then she felt the urge to giggle, thinking, if she isn't speaking to me, she can't very well yell at me, can she?

"Give it another try, Katie," her stepfather urged. "Okay?"

What could she say? He had been kind to her, and this was important to him. And there was always the chance that his "little talk" had changed Paige's attitude.

Right, a devilish little voice inside her head said, and I know an elephant who can dance "Swan Lake."

Well, she could always hope.

It didn't take her long to realize just how futile that hope was. It quickly became obvious that Paige wasn't at all happy about having her Sunday afternoon blown to smithereens. She slumped in a corner of the front seat, leaning against the car door. Her face looked like every stitch of clothing she was wearing was pinching.

If she smiles, Katie thought as she fastened her seat belt, her face will probably crack. "Put your seat belt on, please," she said. Bill had told her very clearly that she was never to start the engine until every passenger had clicked a seat belt securely around themselves.

"*I* give the orders here," Paige retorted hotly. But, after a long moment in which she continued to lean lazily against the door, she did as Katie had ordered, managing to latch the buckle over her suede jacket in spite of her slouched position. "*Now* can we get going, please? I have more important things to do than sit here in the driveway with you."

Yeah, Katie thought, and I'll bet one of them isn't cleaning your side of the room. Paige had come home early the night before. She could have cleaned up her mess before she went to bed. It was disgusting, living with that all of the time. But since this wasn't the right time to bring up the subject of Paige's careless housekeeping, she started the car.

Paige made a real effort to hold her tongue. But each girl was well aware that the other one didn't want to be where she was. The strain set both tempers and teeth on edge. An uneasy silence settled over the car.

A light drizzle began to fall. Three times Katie reached out to turn on the windshield wipers. Three times she hit the light switch instead.

To her complete astonishment, Paige giggled.

"I think," she said, "that you can get a ticket for excessive light-flicking."

In spite of her surprise, Katie laughed.

So the next time Paige said curtly, "Move over. You're hogging half of the other lane," Katie moved over without a word of protest. And when Paige ordered, "Take a left here," Katie took a left. Without a word. But the moment of laughter began to fade. And when Paige said, "For Pete's sake, Katie, pay attention! You almost ran over the curb!" that moment of shared giggling disappeared completely. Katie could feel her muscles tightening up again as Paige went on barking out orders like a drill sergeant.

"Okay, okay," Katie finally said in exasperation. "Where's your chair and whip?"

Paige grunted. "My, aren't we getting testy? This *is* supposed to be a lesson, after all. Don't your teachers at school tell you what do do?"

Katie ignored that. The light drizzle had become a steady rain, decreasing her visibility and increasing the strain on her nerves. The road felt slick under the car's tires, and she wasn't at all confident about being able to handle things if the car should skid.

"Why don't we just go home, Paige?" Katie suggested. The thought of being safe in her own room and out of the car tugged at her.

"We can't go home yet. We haven't been out long enough. Dad will think we had a fight. And he'll blame me."

"Well, I'll just tell him that we didn't."

"He won't believe you." Paige's voice took on

a note of bitterness. "He *always* blames me when we have a fight."

That wasn't true. "Oh, Paige, he does not." But if he did, Katie thought, maybe that's because you work harder at picking fights than I do. She kept that thought to herself.

There was little Sunday afternoon traffic, but that fact failed to lift Katie's spirits. She had already decided that when she got her license (*if* she got her license), she would never drive in bad weather. It was just too hard to see with a curtain of rain pouring across the windshield. And it was getting foggy.

"He doesn't always blame you," Katie said, braking gradually in advance of a Stop sign. "I've been lectured, too. You're just not around when Mom lets me have it. She knows it would be excruciatingly embarrassing if you were a witness."

Paige sniffed audibly.

Katie checked in both directions, peering through the rain-slicked windshield, before switching her foot from the brake to the accelerator. When the car slid slightly to the left as she gave it gas, her heart jumped into her mouth.

"Please, Paige, let's go home. I'm not used to driving in this kind of weather."

"You're not used to driving, period. Oh, all right. But *you* deal with Dad. You make it crystal-clear that cutting the lesson short was your idea!"

Relieved, Katie nodded and turned the car around to head for home.

Although she said nothing, Paige was every bit as relieved as Katie. She wasn't having much luck at holding her tongue, and a fight could break out at any moment. Bill had made it very clear that if she or Katie came storming into the house a second time, use of the new car would be sharply curtailed for Paige, if not stopped altogether. The less time she spent instructing Katie, the less chance there was of trouble developing. Now that they were on their way home, she could relax and plan what to do with the rest of her Sunday. Anticipating calling Ben when she got home, Paige leaned against the passenger's seat with her legs stretched out in front of her. She thought of herself as already being "off-duty" as a driving instructor. Katie was doing okay. Besides, the fewer orders she gave, the less chance there was of blowing this driving lesson.

She stopped watching the road.

Katie was watching it. At least, she was trying, even as rain pelted the windshield with layer after layer of cascading water. She hunched forward over the steering wheel, every muscle in her body rigid with tension. All she wanted to do now was get home. At least Paige had finally shut up. That was something.

The intersection she was approaching was not busy with traffic. She would be making a left-hand turn, but she would, she knew, be protected by a green arrow giving her the right-of-way. Then just a few more blocks, the climb up the hill, and they'd be safely home. Until then, she would pay close attention to what she was doing.

In the distance, she could barely make out several approaching vehicles. But they would have a red light and she would have the green arrow. No problem. She hadn't yet become accustomed to making turns in the face of oncoming traffic, so she was grateful for the arrow. Turning in front of oncoming drivers seemed so risky. How did people learn to judge exactly when there was ample time to turn and when there wasn't? Well, she didn't have to worry about that at this corner, thank goodness.

"Turn the defroster on," Paige said as they waited for their arrow. "I don't know how you can see a thing!"

Katie stared at the control panel on the dashboard. She giggled. "If you'll pardon the pun, I don't have the foggiest notion how any of that stuff works."

Clucking impatiently, Paige came out of her own fog long enough to reach over and flip on the defroster before settling back against the door again.

The windshield cleared quickly. When the green arrow lit up, Katie could see it quite clearly. About time, she thought impatiently, anxious to get home.

As she began her turn, she anticipated some cutting comment from Paige. Which would it be: that she was making the turn too wide . . . or too tight? That she was going too fast . . . or too slow? That she was too tense, or too relaxed?

No comment came. Curious, Katie glanced over at her stepsister. And gasped in horror as she saw, through Paige's window, a large white pickup truck barreling through the intersection against the red light. He was headed straight through the rain for Paige.

Katie screamed. Paige jerked out of her daydream, eyes wide. "What? What?" she cried angrily.

"Move!" Katie screamed, her mind working furiously to think of a way to avoid the truck. "Move! Get down!"

But there was no time. And there was nothing Katie could do but watch in horror as Paige turned her head to the right, following Katie's horrified gaze, just as the truck, in a belated screech of brakes, smashed into the maroon Chevy Virginia Mae Guthrie Whitman had bought for her children.

Paige's thin, high-pitched scream ripped through the air, a sound that Katie would hear in her memory for a long time to come, a sound that was cut short and replaced by the terrible crunch of metal on metal, the shattering of glass, and the scrape of metal on asphalt as the truck pushed the crumpled car across the street and into the curb, where both vehicles came to a grinding halt.

Later, when people asked Katie what the accident was like, she would answer, "I don't know." And she would be telling the truth. Because the horrible sight of Paige's body, held prisoner by the safety belt Katie had insisted upon, bearing the full impact of the collision, blotted out everything else for her. Sharp objects flew through the air, driving themselves through the thick fabric of her pink jacket and piercing her upper arm and right thigh, but she didn't feel it. What she felt instead was the passenger's door being driven into Paige's right side. A heavy object, probably Paige's shoulder bag, thudded against Katie's forehead with a blow so forceful it slammed her head back against the headrest. But she didn't feel it. What she felt instead was the crumpled mass of metal that had been the right side of the car pressing into Paige's flesh, turning her right leg into shredded denim mixed with a sickening bright red.

She remembered that she had been the one to cut the lesson short. She was the one who had insisted they return home. If she hadn't, they wouldn't have been in this particular intersection when the white pickup ran the red light.

Where was her mother? She wanted her mother.

People began gathering around the wreck. Katie wondered dully what they were doing out in such terrible weather. Why weren't they home, safe and dry?

She noticed that the windshield was shattered. And wondered if her mother would be really mad. This was a brand-new car. She wouldn't blame her mother if she never bought another single thing for her daughter. I don't deserve to have nice things, she thought sadly, if I can't take better care of them than this.

Someone rapped on Katie's window. "Roll it down!" someone shouted.

She didn't want to roll the window down. They would all see Paige if she rolled the window down. And Paige looked terrible. Like a rag doll. No life in her. It was as if she no longer had any bones. Her head was folded into her chest, a curtain of black hair covering her face, some of it mixed with the same bright red that was quickly spreading across her right thigh. Paige wouldn't want anyone to see her like that. She would hate that. Katie felt a fierce need to protect Paige from prying eyes. I'll comb her hair first, she thought. If I can just find my purse. Where did I put my purse?

The pounding on the window became more insistent. "Open the window!" someone shouted. "Your door is jammed!"

My door isn't jammed, Katie thought smugly. It's just locked. Why would *my* door be jammed? The truck didn't hit on *my* side. It hit on Paige's side. It hit Paige. And I think it killed her.

The wail of an ambulance sounded in the distance. She unlocked the door because what good would it do to have an ambulance if the ambulance people couldn't get them out of the car? Someone pulled the door open. Arms reached in for her as the ambulance shrieked to a halt and paramedics in uniforms under clear plastic raincoats spilled from the back of it.

"Are you okay?" an elderly man in a tan raincoat, water dripping from the brim of his hat, asked Katie as he peered into her face.

Her legs gave way and she sagged against him. "Over here!" he called to the paramedics, but Katie put a hand over his mouth.

"Shh!" he said. "Don't call them. I'm fine. It's Paige who's hurt. The truck hit her. I was driving, so I didn't get hurt. She's over there, on the other side of the car."

One of the paramedics came toward her, while the others followed Katie's pointing finger.

"You don't look so good yourself," the man in the raincoat said, holding her so she wouldn't fall

37

to the ground. "You let this nice paramedic take care of you, okay?"

Katie looked up into the face of a paramedic, a tall young woman with red hair, carrying a medical bag. And she thought of Megan, who had red hair, too.

"Megan is going to hate me," she said clearly. "Because I just killed her sister."

Then finally, finally, she fainted.

CHAPTER 5

When Katie awoke, she was lying flat on her back with strangers peering into her face. Instead of "Where am I?" she asked in a shaky voice, "Paige? Where's Paige?" Everything around her seemed very white and very cold.

The female stranger, wearing a white coat, turned to the male stranger, dressed identically, and murmured, "Why does she want to know about a page?"

"Girl she was with," the man, who was doing something to a black band around Katie's upper arm, answered. "She's in E.R. Four."

Both of her arms hurt. The black band was too tight and her other arm burned. Something kept pulling at the skin.

"I'm stitching you up," the woman doctor said. "But you're going to be all right. Some bad cuts and a rotten bump on the head, that's all."

"Sister," Katie said. "Where is my sister?"

"Was her sister with her?" The man took off the black band. But the arm still hurt.

"Don't think so. Different last name on the other girl in the car. Probably a pal. Maybe she just wants her sister with her." To Katie, she said, "Sorry, no visitors. This is the emergency room. But you'll be done here soon, and you can see your family then."

When Katie said nothing, the woman continued, "You were luckier than your friend. She took the full impact of whatever clobbered you."

"A truck," Katie murmured. "It was a truck." She felt so sleepy. Had they given her something, some drug? "He ran the red light. There wasn't anything I could do. It wasn't my fault."

"Hey," the man said, patting her shoulder, which hurt, "take it easy, kiddo. No one accused you of anything. We're just here to fix you up."

"And she's not my friend," Katie continued, confusing both doctors, "she's my sister. We're not . . . we're not friends at all." Tears filled her eyes and spilled down her face. "But I never wanted her to get hurt. I *didn't!*"

"Take it easy," the man said again. He turned away from the table Katie was lying on. Returning with a fat roll of adhesive tape and a roll of gauze, he began applying them to Katie's face. It hurt. But she thought it served her right after what she'd done. Maybe she'd be scarred forever, as punishment.

"Is my sister okay?" she persisted. Then the question struck her as ridiculous. How could Paige possibly be okay? That truck had hit right where she was sitting. Her leg . . . then Katie thought, maybe Paige is dead and they won't tell me because they think it would upset me.

She moaned. Hadn't she, just yesterday, toyed with the idea of slamming the car into a wall, hitting the wall on Paige's side? She hadn't done it, and she never, never would have done such a thing, but still. . . .

"Oh, God," she cried out, and the woman asked sharply, "What is it? What hurts?"

How could Katie answer, My conscience? She closed her eyes and said nothing.

"No reason for X-rays," the male doctor said. "We're not even going to keep you here overnight. You'll be sore for a while until your cuts and bruises heal, but you'll be better off in your own home. You're a very lucky girl," he said sternly. "You were smart to have your seat belt on, or you might have gone right through the windshield."

Paige had *her* seat belt on, Katie thought bitterly, and what good did it do her?

Why wouldn't these people tell her how Paige was?

"A nurse will be in shortly to take you to your family. They're waiting for you across the hall." Something resembling a grin crossed his round face. "Don't go away." With a mirthless laugh, he left.

"Sorry about that," the woman said, clipping something with a pair of scissors and standing back to survey her handiwork. "He likes to think he has a sense of humor." She patted Katie's hand briefly and said, "You really are going to be fine. I promise. No scars. Just get plenty of rest and see your family doctor in a week. You'd probably

41

rather have him or her take the stitches out, right?" And she turned to leave.

"Wait!" Katie cried. "What about my sister?"

"She's probably waiting out there with the rest of your family." And the woman was gone, leaving a miserable, guilty, frightened Katie alone in the cold, white room. She wished with all her heart that her family would come in and be with her.

Her family, including Megan and Mary Emily, were huddled together, white-faced and anxious, on a blue vinyl bench in the nearly empty waiting room. An elderly man dozed on a bench opposite them, and a mother comforted her small son who had a bleeding foot. A nurse came and took him into a treatment room, insisting that the mother remain where she was. The boy started screaming at the top of his lungs until his mother promised him a sundae if he would be a "big, brave boy." At that, he let the nurse lead him away, and the room became very quiet.

It was a depressing room, the walls once white had now faded to a grayish-beige. There were no windows to let in light, no posters on the wall, and the floor tiles were the same dingy color as the walls. The room was clean and sparsely furnished with the blue benches, a small table bearing a coffeepot and styrofoam cups, plastic spoons, a bowl with pink and blue sugar packets, and a soda machine. Perhaps those who had designed it knew that the way the room looked would make little difference to the people who waited there.

Virginia Mae clutched her husband's hand so tightly her knuckles were as white as her face. Every few minutes she would murmur, "Please, God, please," and Bill, grim-faced, would pat her hand. The two younger girls held hands, too, concentrating all of their energies on not crying. Tuck sat, looking very much alone, at the far end of the bench, with no hand to hold. "I wish someone would tell us something," he muttered from time to time.

It was Tuck who had taken the terrible call. He hadn't understood the message at first. Megan and Mary Emily were playing a game of Careers with their parents in the living room, and there was a lot of shouting and laughter and cries of, "That's not fair!" Tuck, the telephone clapped to his ear, heard "hospital" and "accident" and "police" and had a hard time putting it all together. When he finally did, his knees gave way, and he sank into a chair beside the telephone, his eyes on his mother.

Virginia Mae and Bill looked up from their game. One glance at Tuck's face brought them up out of their chairs and to his side.

"What is it?" Bill asked.

"It's the girls," Virginia Mae whispered before Tuck could answer. "I know it is! This rain . . . we never should have let them go out on the road today."

"It wasn't raining when they left," her husband reminded her. "Tuck?"

Tuck replaced the receiver. He stood up, facing them. "Now, don't get all bent out of shape, Mom," he said as lightly as he could manage, "but there's been an accident."

His mother gasped, her hands flying to her mouth.

Mary Emily tugged at Virginia Mae's red wool skirt. "Mommy? Mommy, what's the matter?"

Megan said, "Daddy?"

Bill put an arm around Virginia Mae's shoulders. "How bad is it?" he asked Tuck.

"Don't know. They wouldn't say. The woman just said two girls had been brought into the emergency room and one of them had this address and last name in her purse."

Virginia Mae sagged against Bill in relief. "Well!" she said brightly. "If Paige gave them her name and address, it couldn't have been much of an accident, could it? Probably just a fender-bender. I'm sure they're both fine, but we'd better get down there. They'll be anxious to get home."

Tuck hesitated. "Mom . . . the woman didn't say Paige *gave* them her address. She said they found it in her purse."

That shook her, he could see that. But he didn't want her walking into the emergency room totally unprepared. The woman who called had made it sound quite serious.

But Virignia Mae had made up her mind that it was a minor accident, nothing to get all upset about. They'd go straight to the hospital and bring the girls home. They'd be shaken up, of course, and probably scared to death, she told her family as she hurried into the foyer to pull jackets from the coat rack. "But they'll have all

44

afternoon and evening to calm down and rest up. You younger girls come along with us."

That was all right with Megan and Mary Emily. If Katie and Paige were hurt, they wanted to be there to help cheer them up.

Virginia Mae was still chattering brightly about how they could comfort two very frightened girls who had had a traumatic experience.

But her attitude changed very quickly at the hospital, when the first doctor arrived to explain the situation. "Both girls are your daughters?" he asked, seeing only one set of parents in the waiting room.

The Whitmans nodded.

"I can't tell you much right now," he said. "Except that one girl's injuries are relatively minor. The other girl's are not."

One girl? Virginia Mae looked faint. Tuck could see that she couldn't bear to ask which girl had been injured more seriously. But he could, because he wanted to know.

"Which one will be okay?" he asked bluntly.

The doctor, a balding, heavy-set man in a black raincoat, waved his hands impatiently. "I'm sorry, I can't even tell you that yet. I haven't seen them. I just got called in. Wanted you to know that they're being taken care of. Perhaps I shouldn't have said anything until I knew more."

Bill Whitman shook his head. "No, we understand, really. And we want to know everything. We appreciate the little you've told us. Just keep us posted, please."

"Certainly. Try not to worry. I'll get back to you the minute I know more."

And that was the last they'd heard. Knowing that one girl was seriously injured had silenced Virginia Mae. She'd been sitting quietly, white-faced, ever since, except for her occasional, "Please, God, please!"

After what seemed like hours of a tense, strained silence, the doctor finally returned. He was dressed in white now. The family got to its feet in one collective, apprehensive motion.

"I'm sorry it took so long," he apologized. His name tag read, Julius Barton, M.D. "One of your girls is being released as soon as they finish patching her up. Some cuts and bruises. She'll have stitches but no scars. But she's pretty badly shaken up and will need plenty of rest and tender, loving care. But I'm sure I don't need to tell you that."

"And our other daughter?" Bill asked, his voice heavy with dread. But he still didn't ask which girl could be released. Not yet.

"Unfortunately," Dr. Barton said, "your other daughter was not so lucky. I understand her side of the car took the full impact. They're prepping her for surgery right now. Her right leg — "

Tuck could stand it no longer. Leg, he thought, leg. How can someone with a bum leg do competitive swimming? "*Which* right leg?" he cried. "Who is having surgery? Paige? Or Katie?"

The doctor looked stricken. "Oh, I'm sorry! I just assumed the emergency room doctors had already spoken with you. I didn't realize . . ." He glanced down at a clipboard in his hands.

Virginia Mae clung to her husband, scarcely breathing, her eyes on the doctor's face. Megan and Mary Emily, faces as white as their mother's silk blouse, clung to each other. Tuck held his breath.

"The girl who can go home is Katie . . . Summer? Is that right? The one with the more serious injuries is Paige."

Virginia Mae breathed again. "Oh, thank God," she cried, "Katie is all right!" Then, realizing what she had said she turned to her husband, dismay on her face. "Oh, Bill, I'm so sorry! I didn't mean . . ."

"It's all right," he assured her, "really, it is. I'm glad for Katie, too. It's okay." Turning back to the doctor, he asked, "Just how bad is Paige? A broken leg? Fracture, maybe? Nothing that can't be fixed, I'm sure." But he didn't sound sure at all.

Tuck thought, he looks like someone just kicked him in the stomach. He found himself wishing there was some way he could fix everything for Bill, make this awful nightmare go away. But he didn't know how. And he wondered if Virginia Mae knew that if the news had gone the other way, if it had been Katie whose injuries were more serious, Bill would have had exactly that same look on his face. Exactly.

Dr. Barton sat down and motioned to the family to do the same. "It's bad," he said when they were all seated close together opposite him. His eyes behind wire-rimmed glasses were sympathetic. Glancing toward Megan and Mary Emily, he asked Bill, "Should I speak freely? Perhaps your son could take the younger girls to the cafeteria?"

"No," Bill said firmly. "They're old enough to know what's going on. And I would never exclude Tuck from this conversation."

Tuck flashed him a grateful look.

The doctor nodded approvingly. "Good. Because all of you will have to hang together on this one. It's not going to go away tomorrow, or any time soon, unless I miss my guess."

Virginia Mae began crying softly.

"I won't lie to you. Your daughter is in bad shape. It may be touch and go for a few days."

The alarm on Paige's father's face became outright fear. "Touch and go? Are you telling me my daughter might not . . . might not make it? That's ridiculous! She's only sixteen years old! Can't you *do* something?"

"Of course. We'll do everything in our power, and I assure you, that's considerable."

"Exactly what is wrong with my daughter?"

"Head injury, for one thing. Apparently the door . . . well, never mind. That's not important. It looks serious, but only time will tell. We'll keep a close eye on her, I promise you that. The goal is to keep her out of coma, and we're taking every precaution in that area. The problem right now is her leg."

"Her leg?" He saw in his mind Paige running lightly down the stairs, her black hair flowing out behind her. Paige jumping rope at the age of six, Paige riding a bicycle furiously down the hill after her mother died, Paige climbing the big maple tree in the backyard. "Her leg? What? It's broken?'

"This is more than a simple break, Mr. Whitman. The leg was, well, it was pretty badly mangled. We intend to save it, but you must know there is a small chance we'll fail."

A deadly silence fell upon the group. Bill's face drained of all color and tears gathered in his eyes. Virginia Mae held him as tightly as she could, completely unaware of her own tears.

Tuck was stunned. Paige lose a leg? Okay, so she wasn't the athlete Katie Summer was. But she was so . . . so active, always rushing here and there, running into the house and running back out again. The image of Paige as someone crippled simply didn't compute in his brain. No. That just couldn't happen.

"Are you saying," Bill asked slowly and deliberately, his voice husky with shock, "that my daughter might lose her leg?"

A strangled cry came from the direction of the doorway.

Heads lifted to look. There stood Katie Summer, her face under the patchwork of adhesive tape the color of stone. She was leaning on the arm of a young nurse in a starched white uniform. Katie's blue eyes, one of them already beginning to discolor, were filling with horrified tears.

"Is . . . is Paige going to lose her leg? Because of *me*?"

The sight of her standing there, hurt and terrified, brought tears to Tuck's eyes. He brushed them away quickly, embarrassed. But she looked so fragile, so hurt. He wasn't used to seeing her like that. He couldn't stand it.

"*Is* she?" Katie was crying openly now, tears pouring down her cheeks. "*Tell* me!"

Her stepfather stood up and in three quick strides, reached her. And pulled her close against his chest. They stood there like that, Katie sobbing, tears trickling down Bill's cheeks, while the rest of the family watched helplessly.

Tuck thought, I don't think we can survive this. I just don't see how.

CHAPTER 6

When Katie pulled away from the comfort of Bill's arms, she looked at her mother with tear-swollen eyes. Tuck waited for Virginia Mae to say something consoling. He sensed that Katie was waiting for the same thing.

But Virginia Mae was deep in conversation with the doctor. And she wasn't asking about Katie's injuries. She was talking about Paige.

"You can't be serious about her leg being in jeopardy," she protested. "She's only sixteen years old!"

Katie moaned and leaned against Bill.

"We'll do everything we can to save it," the doctor repeated. "But it's severely damaged. Right now we're also concerned about the head injury. We'll operate on the leg as soon as we feel it's safe."

"There must be something you can do right

now," a pale and shaken Virginia Mae insisted. "Surely you don't intend to just sit and wait."

"We have no choice. But we're hardly just sitting and waiting. She's being given excellent care, I promise you. You won't be able to see her for some time, though, so I suggest you all go home and get some rest. We'll call you the moment there's any change."

Paige's stepmother gasped. "Leave?" she cried. "We're not leaving! We wouldn't leave Paige now!"

"Mrs. Whitman," the doctor said sternly, "I just told you, there is nothing you can do for Paige now. Later, she'll require a great deal of time and attention. But right now, you have another daughter who needs your help." He glanced at Katie. "You *can* do something for her. Take her home and see that she gets plenty of rest and a great deal of tender, loving care. She's had a rough time of it, too."

"I don't want to leave," Katie argued. "I want to stay here with Paige."

And who's going to prop you up? Tuck wondered. She looked as weak-kneed as a newborn colt and her skin was putty-colored.

"You see?" Virginia Mae cried, appealing to Bill for support, "Katie wants to stay, too."

"But she mustn't," the doctor said calmly. "Surely you can see that. She's had a terrible shock and she *is* injured. Her medical care includes prompt bed rest, and you must see that she gets it."

Tuck's sympathy switched momentarily from

52

his sister to his mother. He could see how torn she was.

Bill saw it, too. "Look," he said, "I'll take these four home, get Katie Summer settled in bed, and ask Miss Aggie to stay overnight. I'm sure she won't mind under the circumstances. She's probably worried sick. Then I'll come back here and wait with you, Virginia. Since we can't talk you into coming home with us."

Mary Emily who had, along with Megan, been listening silently, reached for her mother's hand. "I want Mom to come with us. I don't *want* her to stay here."

"Don't be so selfish!" Katie snapped. "Paige needs her more than we do."

Her younger sister's lip quivered. In one quick stride, Tuck was beside her, taking the younger girl's still-outstretched hand in his. "It's okay, Mary Emily," he said. "We'll get Miss Aggie to stir us up a pot of her famous hot chocolate. And we'll rent a movie, okay? A comedy. Something really hilarious."

Mary Emily looked doubtful, and Megan broke her silence by saying in a shocked voice, "You don't expect us to *laugh*, do you, Tuck?"

Realizing his mistake, he shook his head. "No, honey, you don't have to laugh. On second thought, maybe we'll skip the movie. You two are probably wiped out, anyway. A good night's sleep is the answer. C'mon, I'll escort you to the parking lot. Bill and Katie will be right behind us. Give Mom a hug."

As they left, the doctor repeated his earlier

statement to their parents. "Mr. and Mrs. Whitman, I know how you feel. But you're not going to do your family, yourselves, or your daughter Paige any good by spending the night in the hospital. Please go home with the rest of your family."

"No," Virginia Mae said. And she turned her back on all of them and walked over to take a seat on one of the benches. Clasping her hands together, she sat silently, staring straight ahead of her. The doctor sighed, shook his head, and left the room.

She hasn't even asked me how I feel, Katie Summer thought. Not once. I thought she'd be so upset when she saw how I look. I thought she might be worried that I'd be scarred. That's just the kind of thing she would worry about. But she never said a word.

As if reading her mind, Virginia Mae looked up then. "Are you all right?" she asked, her voice distant, as if she were speaking to a stranger who had just entered the emergency room.

No, Katie thought, I am *not* all right. But her mother had some really terrible things on her mind. It wouldn't be right to fall into her arms and start sobbing, which was exactly what Katie Summer wanted, needed, to do.

She nodded. "Sure. I'm fine. You'll call the house the second you know about Paige?"

Her mother nodded, and Katie and Bill turned to leave.

They were almost to the door, Katie walking very gingerly because every part of her body hurt, when Virginia Mae's voice trembled across the room. "Katie," she asked softly, "what exactly happened? You *were* paying attention to your driving, weren't you?"

Katie gasped and stopped in her tracks. Bill stopped, too, and whirled to face his wife. "For God's sake, Virginia Mae," he cried angrily, "you heard the policeman. The guy ran a red light! It wasn't Katie's fault."

Virginia Mae nodded dully. "Of course. I know that. I wasn't implying that it was her fault."

Yes, you were, Katie accused silently.

"I just wondered," her mother continued in a dreamy sort of voice, "if there wasn't some way she could have avoided him, so that none of this would be happening."

Bill stared at her.

"No, there wasn't," Katie said slowly and deliberately, her voice choked with unshed tears. "Do you think I would have let him hit us if I'd had any choice?"

"No, of course not, dear. I'm sorry. I'm not thinking very clearly now, I'm afraid. I really didn't mean anything. You go home now and get some rest." And Virginia Mae's attention returned to the hands folded in her lap.

On the way to the car, Bill said, "She's upset, honey. She was terrified for both of you. She didn't mean what she just said."

Katie, her face a mask, said nothing. She let him lead her through the parking garage, wincing in pain each time her bruised right foot hit the cement.

"She shook all the way to the hospital. That's how scared she was," he continued earnestly when they were in the car. "We all know there wasn't anything you could have done to prevent the accident. The policeman made that very clear. Your mom's in shock, that's all. She never meant to imply that you were in any way responsible for the accident."

But that *is* what she implied, Katie thought. That is exactly what she implied. And why not? I *was* driving, wasn't I? Not very well, but I was driving. She sank back against the front seat and closed her eyes.

When Bill had paid his parking fee, he pulled the car out into traffic. Late evening now, and dark, there were almost no cars on the road. Nevertheless, Katie's eyes flew open when the car reached the street. She began to tremble violently and although she reached out, she could find nothing to hang onto to steady herself. Her breath came in ragged gasps.

Feeling the motion of the front seat, hearing her gasps, Bill glanced over. What he saw sent his foot to the brake. The car screeched to a halt.

"Katie, what is it? Are you ill?" Had the doctors missed something, perhaps a broken rib that might now be puncturing a lung? "What's wrong?"

When people can't breathe properly, they can't speak properly, and there were several agonizing moments for Bill before Katie managed to gasp, "I . . . can't . . . do . . . this!"

"What? Can't do what? What is it?" A car behind them honked and Bill motioned impatiently for the driver to go around him

"I . . . can't . . . ride . . . in . . . this . . . car."
Katie reached for the door handle.

Bill grabbed at her sleeve. The accident. Of course. Why hadn't he realized how hard it must be for her to be in a car again so soon? She must be terrified. "Honey, I know it's rough. But we have to get home, and this is the fastest way to do that."

"No!" Katie cried, shaking her head. "I can't! Let me walk, please!"

"Look, I'll go very slowly. I promise. You're perfectly safe. There is no traffic. It's late. Everyone is home, which is where you need to be. And you will be, in just a few minutes."

"I can't!" Her voice rose to almost a scream. "I keep feeling that truck hitting us! Paige was . . . Paige was sitting right where I'm sitting!"

Bill didn't know what to do, a feeling he didn't often have. She might feel safer on a bus, but he could hardly send a person in her state of mind and physical condition home on a bus. Or in a taxi. And how would that help, anyway? Wasn't a taxi just a car, after all?

"Katie," he said firmly, turning her around to face him, "I have to get you home. Slide over here closer to me. That might help. And try hard not to think about what happened. Concentrate on something pleasant. Try to remember that the accident is over, it's all behind you now."

"Not for Paige, it isn't," she said shakily. But she slid over toward him an inch or two and he thought her shaking had subsided somewhat. The pang he felt when Katie mentioned his daughter's name ripped at him, causing him a wave of pain and fear that made him dizzy. But his job right now was to get *this* daughter home, calm her down, and get her into bed as the doctor had ordered. He would do that. And then he would return to the hospital to be with his wife and Paige. What was it the doctor had said about Paige? "It will be touch and go for a few days"? What if . . . no, he couldn't think that way. That way lies terror, he thought and turned back to Katie. "Unfasten your seat belt," he said crisply. "Use the one here, in the middle of the seat. Then you'll be sitting right beside me, and you'll feel safer. Okay?"

She did as he told her without comment. Bill patted her gently and started the car.

When they got home, they found Miss Aggie and Tuck trying desperately to persuade Megan and Mary Emily to go to bed. They had steadfastly refused to do so. "I'm not going to bed until we hear from Mom. I thought you said Daddy and Katie were right behind us? Why aren't they here yet?"

Tuck didn't know, and he banished the thought of another accident as quickly as the possibility entered his mind. "You can't stay up all night," he said testily. "Maybe Dad and Katie decided to stay at the hospital, Now, please, just go to bed."

But they wouldn't budge.

When Bill, white-faced and tight-lipped with worry, walked into the house, Tuck heaved a sigh of relief. The girls would listen to him.

He was right. Although it took several promises on Bill's part to have Miss Aggie wake them the very second they heard anything from the hospital, they reluctantly gave in when he finished his arguments by saying, "The very best way you can help Paige is by going to bed."

Miss Aggie took complete charge of Katie Summer, urging Bill Whitman to return to the hospital, where she could see he wanted to be. As anxious as he was to do just that, he hated to leave Katie. She seemed so shocked and hurt and terrified. He felt compelled to stay long enough to make sure she was safely in bed.

"I'll keep an eye on her," Tuck promised, realizing why his stepfather was hesitating. And he didn't blame him. Katie looked terrible. Why was she shaking like that? And why wouldn't she look at anybody? When the girls and Miss Aggie had hugged her, she'd just stared off into space. And she, one of the great huggers of all time, had kept her arms at her sides, as if she'd forgotten how to use them.

"I'll see that she sleeps," Tuck added, wanting desperately to help.

Bill nodded wearily. "Thanks, Tuck. If she gives you a hard time about it, remind her that it's doctor's orders. I'll stay until she's in bed. Then I've got to get back."

"You can go now," Katie said as Miss Aggie led her away. "I'm fine."

But that was so patently false that Bill chose to wait the few more minutes (hours to him) that it took Miss Aggie to get Katie into bed. Then he went in to tell her good night.

"I'll sleep," she promised, her face a white mask mottled with purple bruise marks, "because I know that's what everyone wants me to do."

"Good girl!" he said, bending to kiss her bandaged forehead. "I'll call, I promise. Don't worry. It'll be okay."

He was almost to the door when she said softly, "Tell Mom I'm really sorry, okay? And that I didn't do it on purpose."

So full of pain for her that he was unable to speak, he whirled, returned to the bed, and bent to hold her. "Stop thinking that way," he said in a husky voice. "Just stop it. No one blames you. Just sleep now, okay? Things will look better in the morning."

Then he got up and hurried out of the room.

CHAPTER 7

In spite of what she had promised Bill, Katie Summer didn't intend to sleep. When Miss Aggie finally finished fussing over her and went away, Katie lay in bed staring up at the ceiling and listening for the ring of the telephone. How could she possibly sleep when she had no idea what was happening to Paige? She would lie awake all night if that was how long it took. When she knew for sure that Paige was going to be all right, she'd go to sleep.

But the emergency room doctor had given her a pill to ease her aches and pains. She fought valiantly, but in vain. Her eyes closed.

Four times during the night she was awakened by the sound in her mind of Paige's bone-chilling scream as the truck collided with their Chevy. Each time, Miss Aggie rushed in to comfort her. And each time Katie pulled away from her nightmare enough to ask if there had been any word from the hospital. The answer was always the same, "No, Katie. Now try not to think about it."

And Katie would try, concentrating instead on Christmas or a camping trip they'd taken in Atlanta when they'd had a wonderful time, or the triumphant feeling she had when she won another swim competition, until sleep overtook her again. But the nightmare kept returning.

The fourth time it happened, she lay chilled with sweat and exhaustion, pretending to let Miss Aggie comfort her. But as soon as the worried housekeeper left the room, Katie Summer got out of bed and sat on the floor in front of the tall, narrow window overlooking the side garden. There was no moon. She couldn't see a thing, but it didn't matter. At least here, on the floor, she would be too uncomfortable to sleep. Sleep meant the sound of that scream again, and she couldn't deal with it. Every bone in her body ached and the cuts on her face and hands stung. Wrapping her comforter around her, she lay her arms on the low windowsill and rested her head on her arms. *Why* didn't the telephone ring? Was Bill afraid to call and tell them about Paige's leg? Was he waiting to tell them some awful news in person?

An even more horrible thought came to Katie's mind. Maybe it wasn't Paige's leg. Maybe it was Paige herself.

Frightened, lonely, and exhausted, Katie Summer waited at the windowsill.

Her stepfather found her there the next morning. He had hurried home from the hospital to shave, change his clothes, and check up on the family. He and the hospital staff had urged a drained Virginia Mae to accompany him, but she had staunchly refused. "I'm not leaving Paige," she had insisted.

And when he said, "Don't you want to check up on Katie?" she answered, "You can do that for me. I'm sure Miss Aggie and the others are taking good care of her. Tell her I send my love and I'll be home just as soon as I can leave Paige."

Remembering Katie's state of mind the night before, Bill felt strongly that a little reassurance from her mother was what she really needed. But there was no changing his wife's mind, so he had left the hospital alone, wishing fervently that he had good news to take with him. He knew no more about Paige's condition than he had the night before: It remained unchanged.

When he walked into the older girls' bedroom a short while later and found Katie Summer, her face bruised and swollen, huddled on the floor by the window, he felt a sudden, fierce anger toward her mother. It was fleeting, and disappeared as quickly as it had come, but it startled him. Virginia Mae was keeping a vigil for *his* daughter. How could he possibly feel anger toward her?

Assuring himself that it wasn't anger he had felt at all, just fierce pity for Katie, he went to wake her. He hated to, sensing that she probably hadn't had much rest. But he didn't have much time, and Katie would be unforgiving if he left without speaking to her, although he had little information to give her. Still, he had promised.

He woke her gently. He could see as she opened her eyes that she had no idea where she was or what her stepfather was doing kneeling on the floor in front of her. That meant that unless she remembered last night's events on her own, he would have to refresh her memory, a painful task that he wasn't sure he was up to at this moment.

A sleepy Katie couldn't imagine why Bill was looking at her that way. And what on earth was she doing on the floor? And then, glancing up at the empty bed across from hers . . . where was Paige?

"Oh, no," she cried softly, remembering. Her eyes shifted anxiously to Bill's face. "The accident . . . is Paige okay? Why aren't you at the hospital? Where's Mom? Something terrible has happened, hasn't it?" Before he could stop her, she jumped to her feet, forgetting her own injuries, and screamed in pain. She would have fallen to the floor if he hadn't caught her. "They've amputated Paige's leg, haven't they? *Haven't* they? That's why you're here!"

"No, no, no," he said, sitting her gently down on her bed. "Stop this now, you're getting hysterical. They haven't done anything to Paige. Did you sleep here by the window all night?"

"Yes. No. I don't know. Just please tell me how Paige is?"

"The same." He wished desperately that he could give Katie better news. She looked so frantic, sitting there frightened half to death, the comforter trailing around her blue flowered pajamas. But there was no point in lying. "She hasn't regained consciousness yet."

Katie moaned softly.

"But I'm sure she will, soon," he added quickly, sitting down beside her. "Paige is young and strong and healthy, you know that. I wish you'd try to relax, Katie. It's not good for you to get so upset."

"Is Mom here?"

He saw the hope in her eyes. "No, honey, she's still at the hospital. I tried to talk her into coming with me, but you know your mother when she makes up her mind."

"Oh, that's okay," Katie said, trying and failing to hide her disappointment. "I'm glad she stayed with Paige. It would be awful for her to be in the hospital all by herself."

"Yes, I'm sure it would, although right now Paige isn't really aware of who is there and who isn't." And you *are*, he thought. "Listen, Katie," he said instead, "I think you should know that the accident was mentioned on the news this morning. I heard it on the car radio on my way home."

He hadn't thought it was possible for Katie to become any paler than she already was. "You mean everybody knows what I did?" she whispered, clutching at his jacket lapel like someone grabbing a life preserver.

"Katie. Listen to me." He took her face in his hands, forcing her to look at him. "The accident was *not* your fault. You must know that, because you were there. You *saw* the truck run the red light."

"It all happened so fast. . . ."

"No! No, listen to me! You were not at fault. It

would have happened if Paige had been driving, or if I had, or Mom, or Tuck. That's the truth, Katie."

But he could see she wasn't convinced. And he was losing precious moments. He had to get back to the hospital. He would simply have to deal with this later. Maybe all Katie needed was a little time. "I just wanted to warn you," he said, "the phone will probably be ringing off the hook all day. I'm sure you don't feel like talking to anyone just yet. Why don't we have Miss Aggie and Tuck take the calls? You can return yours when you're feeling better."

"I want to go back to the hospital with you."

"No. Absolutely not. That's impossible. You're in no shape to go anywhere. And you need sleep. I'm going to give you another one of those pills the doctor prescribed." His voice became very stern. "And I expect to hear from Miss Aggie later that you slept. Okay? That's the best thing you can do for Paige and your mom and me right now."

"But — "

"Please, Katie. Do this for me. Go back to bed and get some rest. Your mom and I are going to need your help until Paige gets better. You can't help if you're sick."

Putting it that way did the trick. Katie couldn't refuse a request for help. She nodded. "All right. But tell Miss Aggie not to let me sleep all day, please? I want to know what's going on."

Agreeing, Bill gave her the medication and made sure she was safely in her bed before leaving.

He had been right about the telephone. Word of the accident spread quickly. Because Miss Aggie was busy keeping Megan and Mary Emily occupied, Tuck situated himself by the phone. The most difficult call came from Judy Belnap. She was in tears of shock and dismay throughout the conversation. Rumors exaggerating Paige's condition were flying, and Judy had heard every one of them.

Finally, in desperation, Tuck said, "Listen, would you like to come over here and wait?" After all, she was Paige's best friend. This must be really hard on her. "That way, you'll know the facts as soon as we do."

"Oh, Tuck, that really would help. You sure I won't be in the way?"

He was glad he'd invited her. "No, you won't be in the way. Just come on over. We'll wait this out together."

She thanked him profusely and hung up.

Maybe, he thought as he waited for the phone to ring again, maybe Judy can help with Katie. I know she likes her. More than Paige does. And this is going to be a long day for Katie. It might be nice for her to have a friend her own age here. It occurred to him then that when girls were in trouble, they needed other girls to talk to. But when guys were having a hard time, they almost never turned to each other. That struck him as decidedly weird. And a little sad. Why did guys always think they had to tough things out alone?

Before he could come up with any answer to that question, the phone rang again. He answered it just as Katie, pale and drawn came into the kitchen. She was dressed in old jeans and a faded pink sweatshirt. Her feet were bare, one of them, he noticed, swollen and black-and-blue. He waved her to a chair and finished his phone conversation quickly. She looked so shaky, he was afraid she'd pass out on him, landing on the white tiles in a heap.

"Sit!" he commanded, pulling the chair out for her. "Let's see, you need to . . . eat! Yeah, that's it! Food, the answer to everything. A sandwich, some hot soup maybe. I'll get right on it."

Katie said nothing. She sat in the chair with her hands folded in her lap, an expression of such bleak despair on her face that Tuck knew soup and a sandwich wouldn't do the trick. But he had to do something. Food seemed better than nothing.

Slicing tomatoes at the kitchen counter, he tried to make conversation with his sister. But she interrupted him three times in ten minutes to ask if he was absolutely positive the hospital hadn't called. Each time he answered patiently, "No, not yet," and each time her look of despair deepened.

He knew what she was thinking. She was blaming herself. It was written all over her adhesive-taped face.

"Listen to me," he said gently, placing her sandwich in front of her. "Listen. The accident wasn't your fault. I was the one who talked to the cop on the telephone. He said that idiot never even slowed down, that there was no way you could have avoided him. So quit walking on hot coals about it. Eat your lunch!"

He ladled hot chicken noodle soup into a bowl and placed it in front of her. The phone had ceased its interminable ringing, at least temporarily, and they sat in silence for several minutes. Then Katie lifted her head and whispered, "*Mom* thinks it was my fault." Quiet tears slid down her cheeks. Tuck wondered how much more she could take. So many cuts and bruises, so many tears, and so much pain. Would she ever again be like the Katie he knew?

"No, she doesn't," he protested. "Mom doesn't think that at all. She knows what happened. We all do."

Katie Summer shook her head. Swiping at her nose with the back of her hand, she said softly, "I could tell at the hospital. She practically came right out and said it was my fault."

"She was upset, Katie, that's all." His voice deepened. "I *know*," he said firmly, "that she doesn't blame you. So get that idea right out of your head. And *eat*!"

He sensed that he hadn't been very convincing. And he would bet anything that their stepfather had already had this conversation with Katie. Anyone could see that she was torturing herself with guilt. And whatever Bill had said in response, it hadn't worked. Well, maybe there weren't any words to help Katie Summer right now. He guessed that if there were, they needed to come from Virginia Mae, not from him or Bill. And Virginia Mae wasn't around right now. So it would have to wait.

The doorbell and the telephone rang simultaneously. "I'll get the phone," he said, "you get the door, okay? It's probably Judy. I told her she could come over."

Katie stared at him in dismay. She didn't want to see anyone. She couldn't talk to Judy. Not now, not today. Judy was Paige's best friend. She probably didn't even want to speak to Katie.

Then she took a deep breath and sat up straighter in her chair. Stop thinking of yourself, she scolded. You're supposed to be helping out around here, not feeling sorry for yourself. Judy is Paige's friend, and she must be worried sick. She has a right to be here, so go let her in.

She got up and went to answer the door.

CHAPTER 8

When Katie pulled open the big wooden door, she found Ben Collins and Jake Carson standing on the porch. They had heard about the accident. And she realized, watching their expressions change from mild concern to shock, that she looked worse than they'd expected.

Jake immediately stepped forward to fold his arms around her. "Oh, Katie," was all he said. But even needing comfort as desperately as she did, she decided Ben might need it more when he'd heard the details of Paige's condition, and she pulled away from Jake.

She gave Ben the unpleasant details right there on the porch, not wanting to go through it again in front of the family. "We haven't heard any more yet," she finished, her voice apologetic. The shock and confusion in Ben's usually placid face tore at her heart. But she had no words to ease his worry. She waved both boys on inside the house.

"Mom and Bill are still at the hospital. They'll call the minute they know anything."

Inside, they all sat quietly at the kitchen table. Jake and Ben were trying to digest the information Katie had given them, trying to accept the fact that Paige was fighting for her life.

When the doorbell rang a second time, Katie, restless from sitting, went to answer it. This time, it was Judy.

Like Ben and Jake, she was shocked by Katie's appearance. It wasn't just her physical appearance: the sloppy old clothes, the blonde hair hanging limp and lifeless around her swollen face. That was bad enough, so unlike a usually fastidious Katie Summer. It was more than that, Judy decided as she was led into the kitchen. This girl walking in front of her, shoulders slumped and head down, had had her spirit smashed as badly as the new Chevy. That stupid idiot who had run the red light had done a real job on Katie. Gone was her bounce, her beautiful smile, that way she had of being up when everyone around her was down. Not that I blame her, Judy thought, greeting the boys in the kitchen. But I sure hope it doesn't last. I'll bet even Paige would miss the old Katie, although she'd never admit it, not in a million years.

"Heard anything?" she asked Tuck, knowing even as she asked what the answer would be. The atmosphere in the big house was still definitely one of painful waiting. She could feel it.

The next time the telephone rang, it was Katie's best friend, Lisa. "Sara and Diane are here with me," she told Katie in a voice filled with concern.

72

"And we want to come over. It must be really rough on you, waiting to hear about Paige. We thought maybe we could cheer you up."

Katie appreciated their support. But there was no way they could cheer her up. And they'd feel bad about failing. Then she'd feel guilty because they felt bad. The last thing in the world I need right now, she thought, is more guilt. So she turned down their offer, thanking Lisa for making it.

"Ben and Jake and Judy are here," she explained, "so I'm not alone. And I just don't feel like company right now."

"We're not company," Lisa protested. "We're your best friends." Then, a second later, she added, "But we understand. I guess it wouldn't be a good idea to have a crowd there right now. But call us the minute you hear anything, okay?"

Katie promised. And when she hung up, she felt just a little bit less alone.

The afternoon went by at a turtle's pace. Judy tried to read quietly in a corner of the kitchen. Ben and Jake worked outside in the yard, pausing periodically to check with someone in the house. Told there had been no word, they would return to their leaf-raking.

Inside the house, each time the phone rang Katie glanced up anxiously, as did Judy. But Tuck's calm, well-mannered voice told them it wasn't the hospital calling.

Shortly after four o'clock, Megan and Mary Emily, unusually subdued, came into the kitchen for a snack just as the telephone rang. Jake and Ben had just come in, too. A weary Tuck picked up the receiver and said hello. All eyes were on him as he jumped up from the stool, saying, "Mom? Is that you?" Everyone in the room stood up, eyes wide with fear.

Katie grabbed Jake's hand, her breathing uneven. "How is she? How is Paige? Is she okay?" Katie clapped a hand over her mouth to keep from crying out.

Miss Aggie entered the room and, sensing what was happening, put an arm around each of the younger girls' shoulders.

"Yeah. Yeah. Right. Okay."

It was impossible to tell from Tuck's cryptic exclamations what was going on, and Katie bit her lip in frustration. She wanted on the one hand for Tuck to hurry up and tell them what was happening. On the other hand, she wanted him to stay on the phone long enough to find out *everything* that was happening.

"You're sure? So will you guys be home soon or what? What should I tell Miss Aggie? Should she stay tonight?"

There was another long moment of silence as Tuck listened. Katie clutched Jake's hand so tightly her arm ached. It was clear that Paige hadn't died, or Tuck wouldn't be standing there talking so calmly. That took a moment to sink in — Paige had *not* died. She was alive!

"Okay, Mom. So take it easy, okay? Talk to you later." Tuck replaced the receiver and quickly turned to face seven white-faced, barely breathing, very anxious people.

"She's regained consciousness," he announced without delay. "No more danger of coma." He laughed a shaky laugh. "She even asked Mom if they had cut off all her hair."

Katie burst into tears of relief. Megan and Mary Emily cheered. Miss Aggie folded her hands in a prayer of thanks. And Judy hugged Ben and Jake at the same time.

Tuck let them enjoy the moment. Then he raised his hands, saying, "Okay, everybody, that's the good news."

They sobered instantly.

"Now, the bad news. They're still not sure about the leg."

Katie gasped.

"Well, now," Tuck said calmly, "don't go getting all upset again. They seem to be really optimistic, Mom said. The doctors, I mean. They've called in this really terrific orthopedic surgeon from New York." Tuck's eyes fastened on Katie's. "I mean, according to Mom, this guy could piece together a plate-glass window shattered by a hurricane and you'd never be able to spot the seams. He's operating on Paige tomorrow morning at eight o'clock."

But Katie looked so shaken that he quickly added, "They're coming home for dinner, though. Mom wants to shower and change before she goes back to the hospital. *If* she goes back. I heard Bill in the background telling her she should stay home and get a good night's sleep. She didn't sound very enthusiastic about that idea. He said Paige would be sleeping and wouldn't even know Mom was there." Tuck glanced around the room. "Maybe we can all talk her into staying home tonight. Let's give it a try, okay?"

Katie felt torn. She wanted her mother home with a fierce yearning that took her breath away. But if Virginia Mae felt just as strong a need to be with Paige, it wouldn't be right to frustrate her wishes, would it?

"So Paige could still lose her leg?" she asked, her voice flat. She hated herself for tossing such an ugly thought into a room that had only moments before been hopeful, but she couldn't help it. It had to be said, didn't it?

Tuck frowned. "Oh, well, Mom didn't mention that possibility, but . . ."

"Now, you mustn't think that way." Miss Aggie rescued him. "Paige without the use of her two good legs? Why, that's just unthinkable! You put that thought right out of your heads. It won't ever happen, not in *this* lifetime."

A tiny bit of color returned to Megan's face.

"Now all of you skedaddle out of my kitchen, so I can make something special for your folks. Goodness, they haven't had a decent meal since yesterday afternoon. I'd best get busy. Go on, now, take your long faces out of here!"

As they left the room, she called after them, "And see about cheering up, the lot of you! It won't do your folks any good to be around a bunch of Gloomy Gusses."

They knew she was right. And Judy echoed Miss Aggie's sentiments as she was leaving. "I *know* Paige will be okay. Your folks wouldn't be coming home for dinner if they didn't think it was safe. So quit worrying, okay?" To Tuck, she said, "My mom says I have to go to school tomorrow, so I'll call you from there after fourth period and see if you've heard anything yet. Would that be okay?"

Tuck nodded. "Sure. And thanks for coming over."

"Thanks for letting me. I'm glad I was here when your mom called. Tell your folks I said hi, okay?" And she left, thinking what a shame it was that nice, good-looking Tuck only had eyes for Jennifer Bailey, who was semi-attached to Ed Thomas. If Tucker Guthrie would just open his eyes and look around, he might discover that there were other girls at Harrison High. Some of them, in fact, were very close at hand. Some of them, for instance, might even be spending a lot of time in Tucker Guthrie's kitchen.

Shrugging unhappily, Judy went home.

When Katie walked Jake to the door, he tugged gently on her hand to lead her out onto the porch. The air was cool, with twilight fast approaching. The first headlights of the evening snaked up the hill below them. Jake led Katie to the swing.

"And you?" he asked, slipping an arm around her shoulders. "How are you holding up?"

Katie burst into tears.

Jake reached out to pull her in against his chest, saying softly, "I guess that answers my question." He held her silently for a while, letting her cry out some of her fear and anger and guilt. When her sobs had subdued to random sniffles and gasps, he handed her a crumpled tissue unearthed from his jacket pocket, "It's all I've got," he apologized. "It'll have to do."

Leaning against him, Katie heaved one deep, shuddering sigh as she wiped her eyes. "I'm sorry," she whispered.

"Do not, repeat, do *not* apologize. Maybe that's why I brought you out here."

She looked up at him, puzzled.

"I saw the effort you made to quit crying in the kitchen," he explained. "Didn't seem healthy to me. If anybody has a right to hysterics, it's you."

"No." She shook her head. "It's Paige."

"Paige is being taken care of. It's you I'm worried about. Now, just relax for a few minutes. Put all this bad stuff out of your head and pretend we're on a desert island, just the two of us, okay? Orders from Doctor Jake Carson."

Katie managed a weak smile. "Doctor? I thought law was your chosen field, not medicine."

He kissed her on the forehead. "Right now you need T.L.C., not legal advice."

"T.L.C.?"

"Yeah. Tender, loving care. And I'm here to see that you get it. My prescription includes," tipping her chin up toward him, "the following well-accepted medical practice." He kissed her, gently at first, then, as she responded, more firmly. And then repeated his prescription.

"Funny," she said softly as she rested against his chest, "but it really seems to work. I do feel better." She grinned up at him. "But I don't want you to market your miracle cure."

He returned the grin. "No? You don't think I could make a fortune and retire at an early age?"

Katie laughed. "Sure, you could. But this is one cure I'd rather keep for myself."

He bowed from the waist. "Your personal physician, ma'am, at your service." And when she had stopped laughing, he kissed her again.

When Jake left, Katie felt better, enough to allow herself excitement over her parent's impending arrival. She needed desperately to see her mother. More than that, she needed to see for herself that there was no accusation of guilt in Virginia Mae's gray-blue eyes when she looked at Katie. In spite of what Tuck had told Katie, she wouldn't be able to relax until she saw that with her own eyes.

But she didn't see it. Not because her mother looked at her accusingly, but because her mother hardly looked at her at all. And when she did, her eyes were veiled with a thick layer of preoccupation. Her mind was on Paige, and she wasn't really seeing anything.

She's still at the hospital, Katie realized with a wave of bitter disappointment. Virginia Mae had given the younger girls a brief hug, nodded toward Tuck, and asked about Katie's cuts and bruises. Then she had asked Miss Aggie about dinner before going upstairs to take a shower and change her clothes.

And when she came back down and took her place at the dinner table, Katie could see that as far as Virginia Mae was concerned, the dining room had been replaced in her mind by a hospital room. That's where her mother's mind was.

"Sweetheart," Bill said to his wife at one point,

"you haven't touched a thing. Better eat up. Tomorrow's going to be a long day."

Virginia Mae's eyes filled with tears. "I'm sorry. Just a bit tired, I guess. But I'm not at all hungry, isn't that funny? If you'll all excuse me, I think I'll just go rest on the couch for a few minutes. Bill, you come and get me the very second you've finished eating, please. We've been away from the hospital quite a while."

Her husband looked up, his mouth tense. "Virginia, I really am against our returning to the hospital tonight. We're both exhausted. Paige won't even know we're there, you know that."

"But *I* will," Virginia Mae replied in a level voice. "*I'll* know I'm there. You promised."

"I didn't promise. I said I would think about it because it was the only way I could get you out of that hospital. I have thought about it, and it just makes no sense to stay there all night when we could be getting some sleep."

"I'll sleep at the hospital."

"No, you won't. You never closed your eyes last night, not once."

'Well, I will tonight."

Tuck murmured to Katie, "Arguing is not a spectator sport, so let's go."

She stayed where she was. It was important to her to understand why Virginia Mae was arguing, why she was so determined to return to the hospital. If I can understand that, she told herself, then maybe I'll understand why Mom is acting as if no one but Paige exists in this world.

"Virginia Mae, please," Bill pleaded. He lowered his voice. "Hasn't it crossed your mind that since one member of your family is being very well cared for, this might be a good time to pay some attention to the rest of the family? They've had a rough time of it, too, and we won't get another chance like this for the next few days."

Katie squirmed with embarrassment. He meant her, she knew. He was remembering how upset she'd been that morning. He wanted her mother to talk to her, to make her feel better.

Only her mother didn't feel like it.

"It's okay, Dad," Katie said brightly, getting up from the table. "We're fine here, honest. You and Mom go ahead." She picked up her dishes. It suddenly seemed absolutely necessary that she leave that room because no matter how hard she tried, it was impossible to understand why her mother refused to listen to Bill's arguments. They made so much sense.

In the kitchen, Miss Aggie was click-clucking her disapproval over the tension in the house. She had been with the Whitmans long enough that she felt free to speak her mind. "No time to be arguing," she sputtered as Katie arrived with her dishes. "Family in pain needs to stick together, that's all. That's *all!*"

But the argument continued in the dining room. William Whitman used every persuasive tool at his disposal, and he possessed many. But, Tuck thought as he began to climb the stairs, he's up against a *mother* this time.

In the end, Virginia Mae did go to the hospital, and Bill went with her.

Katie decided it was just as well. She hated it when her parents argued. It terrified her. They did it rarely, but sometimes she worried that that was only because they hadn't been married very long. She never knew exactly why her own father had walked out on his family. Her mother never talked about it. But his departure, for whatever reason, was proof to Katie that marriages didn't always last. And if anything like that ever happened with Virginia Mae and Bill, she would die. She told herself constantly that it would never happen, because that was what she needed to tell herself. Although they were arguing now, they *were* happy together. Anyone could see that.

It's all because of the accident, she thought. *My* accident.

Shivering, she crawled into bed, pulling her comforter up around her neck.

CHAPTER 9

The next day was only slightly less agonizing. Katie, weary from lack of sleep, paced nervously in the kitchen, unable to eat. Megan, Mary Emily, and Tuck had all refused to attend school and were waiting with her. Yet Katie felt very much alone. Miss Aggie continually urged her to "take some nourishment, child!" but the very thought of food sent her stomach into rebellion. She wanted very much to call Lisa or Sara or Diane, but they were at school, unavailable to her.

It was ten o'clock. Paige had already been in surgery for two solid hours. What was taking so long? Maybe those doctors didn't know what they were doing. Doctors weren't infallible. They made mistakes. What if they made one now?

No, that couldn't happen. The image of Paige being permanently handicapped was all wrong.

Shortly after ten, Jake arrived, bearing a huge bouquet of flowers for Katie. "I didn't buy them," he admitted as she buried her face in the yellow and rust blooms. "Mr. Danzig over on Cherry Lane has a greenhouse. He heard about the accident and thought these might help cheer everyone up."

"They're beautiful," Katie murmured. Virginia Mae would like them. If she ever came home again.

"Ben's coming, too. I talked to him earlier. He had to go to school for a while, but he'll be here in a little bit. You know he's really scared to death for Paige."

Katie nodded. "I know. We all are." The phone screamed. Katie leaped out of her chair and grabbed it.

"Dad? Is it over? How is she? Did they. . . ?"

No one in the cheerful, sunny kitchen drew a breath. Jake came up behind Katie to put his hands on her shoulders.

She listened. Then she sagged against Jake. But before any of them could cry out, thinking the worst, she gasped, "No, no, it's okay! It's okay! They saved her leg!"

Tuck took the phone from her. "Bill? Fill me in." And Katie turned to let herself be held against Jake's chest. Miss Aggie cried, and Megan and Mary Emily hugged each other. Ben arrived a few moments later, greeted at the door by a teary-eyed but smiling Miss Aggie. The mood in the kitchen when he entered was vastly different from the day before and his relief was evident.

"So!" he exclaimed heartily in a futile attempt to hide the emotion that was overwhelming him,

"I'm not going to have to push her around in a wheelchair after all. That's good news!"

""Ben!" Katie scolded through her tears of relief, "that's a horrible thing to say!" But she was too happy to be really angry.

Jake laughed. "You sure have a way with words, Collins."

Ben took a seat at the table. "Look, let's face it," he said with a grin, "Paige Whitman would *not* make a good semi-dependent person. That's why I knew it would never happen. Never."

But they all knew he'd been every bit as worried as they had.

"Look, everyone," Tuck said soberly when they'd all had time to calm down, "Paige may be out of the woods, but Bill said she's going to have a pretty rough time of it. That leg is in a bad way. She'll be in the hospital for a while. And when she comes home, she's going to need intensive physical therapy. We're all going to have to chip in and help."

Katie Summer's enormous relief went into self-destruct. Why hadn't she realized that the surgery was just the beginning of a long haul for all of them? Judging from Tuck's words, life was going to center around Paige's physical problems for some time to come.

"Katie," the housekeeper said, "now that we've had good news, let me fix you something to eat. Some nice scrambled eggs, maybe?"

Katie shook her head. The appetite that had surfaced just moments earlier sank. "I . . . I just think I'll go upstairs and rest for a while, if nobody minds. I didn't get much sleep last night."

Surprised by the sudden change in her mood, everyone stared at her. She stood up, lifting her chin with determination. "If Mom calls again while I'm upstairs," she said in a clear voice, "you tell her she can count on all of us to help as much as we can. I'll . . . I'll quit the swim team. I'll come straight home from school. With Mom at the hospital a lot, there will be lots to do around the house."

Miss Aggie sputtered, "You'll do no such thing! My goodness, your folks wouldn't like that at all. They're real proud of your swimming. I can handle things here just fine. You quit worrying!"

"Then," Katie added, "I'll just go to the hospital every day after school. That will give Mom a break. And when Paige comes home, we will *all* have to help. She'll need things. And she'll be bored."

"I want to help, too!" Megan cried. "She's my sister, too!"

"Me, too!" Mary Emily echoed.

"We'll all help," Tuck said. "But for right now, why don't we relax? The call from Bill was good news, right? Maybe we should just take it easy this afternoon. The last two days have been rough. How about if Megan, Mary Emily, and I take a hike to the park? Katie Summer can rest and you guys," addressing Jake and Ben, "might as well get back to your regular routines. And if either of you is interested," grinning at Ben, "Paige might be able to have visitors in a day or two."

Katie watched as first Ben's, then Jake's expression brightened. She was happy for Ben. But she couldn't deny the tiny pang of jealousy that went through her as she looked at Jake. A flush of shame quickly followed the stab of jealousy. What was wrong with her? She shouldn't be thinking of herself right now. The only thing that mattered now was Paige's recovery. She would need every friend she had to help her through that. Including Jake. He had been there for her when *she* needed him. It was only fair that he should be there for Paige, too.

"Oh, Miss Aggie," Tuck said as Ben and Jake got up to leave, "Mom and Bill are coming home for dinner. I guess Bill's going to have to rope and tie Mom to get her out of there, but he said to tell you to count on them."

The younger girls cheered again. Even Katie brightened a little. Maybe now that the worst, the most terrible part, was over, she'd have a few precious moments alone with her mother. She'd settle for just a few moments. That wasn't so much to ask, was it?

But she didn't get it. Not that evening. Because her mother came home from the hospital totally drained. Each of them got a warm hug before she excused herself and went upstairs.

Katie understood. She did, at least enough to overcome her disappointment. It had been a ghastly two days for her parents. They were exhausted. Her stepfather tried to make up for Virginia Mae's absence at the dinner table but he, too, was worn out. After explaining to them, gently and briefly, what was in store for Paige, he gave in to his own fatigue. At Miss Aggie's urging he went to bed.

When Katie and the others had finished helping Miss Aggie clean up after dinner, Katie stayed in the kitchen alone. It was time she returned a few telephone calls. Not that it was an unpleasant chore. As tired as she was, she desperately needed to talk to someone. She would have preferred that that someone be her mother. But this time, she'd just have to settle for Sara or Diane or Lisa.

They were all glad to hear from her. Diane wanted to come right over, but Katie explained that everyone was exhausted and company probably wasn't a good idea. Sara promised to collect all of Katie's school assignments and Lisa said that everyone at school, including the swim coach, had been asking about Katie and Paige.

It was Lisa who, innocently enough, sent Katie Summer to bed in a fresh wash of tears.

"Poor Paige," she said after making sure that Katie was in acceptable health. "My dad says her leg will probably never really be okay again."

Which wouldn't have carried quite as much weight except for one thing: Lisa's father was a doctor, a specialist in Athletic Medicine. So if *he* said that Paige's injured leg would never be normal, it was probably true.

Unable to continue the conversation, she excused herself, claiming a headache. Then she ran upstairs to her room, locked the door, and threw herself across her bed.

Which gave her an unobstructed view of Paige's cluttered but unoccupied bed. She couldn't stand looking at it. Jumping up, she ran to the door, unlocked it, threw it open and ran to Tuck's room. She rapped on his door, heedless of sleeping family members.

'What? What is it?" Tuck cried, opening the door in his pajamas, his curly hair rumpled. "Has something happened at the hospital?"

"No, no, I'm sorry. I didn't mean to scare you." She should have known he'd think that something had happened to Paige. "I'm sorry. Can I come in? Please? Just for a second."

Tuck was as worn out as he'd ever been. The need for sleep tugged vigorously at him. But he could see Katie's need, too. And he sensed that she was reluctant to bother Virginia Mae just now. He could at least listen to his sister.

He invited her in and closed the door, and she took a seat on his unmade bed. He listened without comment as she began talking about how distant their mother seemed.

"She's just tired, Katie," he told her. "We all are. It's been a rough couple of days." He'd never seen Katie so down. But the words she wanted to hear wouldn't really do her much good coming from him. He knew she needed to hear them from their mother.

"The trouble is," Katie said slowly, "it's all just beginning. You know that, don't you?" She sat cross-legged, looking, Tuck thought, like a lost child. "You heard Dad. Paige will be in the hospital for a while. Mom will probably camp out at her bedside. Not that I blame her," she added hastily as he opened his mouth to speak. "I know it will be horrible for Paige. But it's just going to be so weird around here without Mom. And then, even when Paige gets home, she'll still need lots of care."

"Yeah, so Bill said. But we can deal with that." Tuck just wanted to go to sleep and close out the accident. They hadn't exactly been one big happy family *before* the accident. He shared Katie's worry about one thing: what was it going to be like now? But if he admitted he was concerned, Katie might just fall apart.

"Well?" She looked at him expectantly. "Don't you think it's going to be rough? I mean, you saw how Mom was tonight. Like she wasn't really here."

Because he didn't know what to say to comfort her, Tuck became impatient. "Katie, what do you expect? I mean, she's been at the hospital ever since the accident! No wonder she's spaced out. Give her some time to pull herself together, okay?"

Katie's face flushed scarlet. Tuck was instantly sorry. He'd been too rough on her. In her present state of mind, she needed kindness, not criticism.

But it was too late. Katie rose from the bed as if her body were being directed by a puppeteer. "You're right," she said hoarsely. "I'm just being selfish. Especially since all of this is my fault."

And before he could think of words to stop her, she was gone, closing the door softly behind her.

In her room, Katie lay on her bed with her eyes closed for a long time. After a while, she decided that she wasn't going to shed one more tear. Not one. Enough of that. It didn't do any good at all and it gave her a headache. As much as Tuck's words had hurt her, she decided he'd been right. This whole thing was much harder on Mom than anyone else, except maybe Paige. And there she'd been, sitting on Tuck's bed complaining because her mother wasn't paying any attention to her. No wonder Tuck had been disgusted.

She would make it up to her mother. And to Paige. Somehow. She opened her eyes and turned her head toward the empty bed. She wouldn't complain anymore, no matter how busy her mother got. She would help Miss Aggie cook and clean and do laundry. Anything she could do to make up for this awful thing that had happened to her family, she would do.

And she would begin, she decided, staring at Paige's corner of the room, by creating order out of the chaos she saw there. When Paige came home, she would come home to a spotless, organized half of a room.

She would begin first thing the following morning.

CHAPTER 10

The first thing Katie Summer did after waking up was hide her learner's permit in the bottom of her sweater drawer. She had no intention of ever using it again.

Then she threw on old jeans and a faded sweatshirt, wrapped a rubber band around her hair without even bothering to brush the strands more than a few half-hearted licks, and went downstairs.

The kitchen was quiet when she descended the stairs shortly after nine o'clock. Miss Aggie explained that Mr. Whitman had called from the hospital to suggest that the two younger girls go back to school.

"They had conniption fits," the housekeeper confided, bustling about the room putting dishes away. "But your dad said there was no point to keepin' them home and I agreed. They're better off in school keeping busy." She glanced over toward Katie, who was unenthusiastically buttering a piece of toast. "You should go back, too, Katie. Tuck went this morning. Nothing you can do here. And there's your swimming. You don't want to get behind in that."

"Oh, I'm giving that up," Katie announced, trying to seem casual.

"Oh, Katie, no! You mustn't do that!"

"Oh, it's okay. I was getting tired of it, anyway. The routine and the drudgery of it can be a real drag sometimes. Anyway," she said, wiping the counter with a dampened paper towl, "Mom's going to need all the help she can get around here. I can't be out of the house until six or seven every night."

Miss Aggie frowned. "Your mother won't like this. Not one little bit. She's real proud of your swimming."

"I know." Katie kept her tone of voice light. "But she'll be glad when she sees how much help I can be. Besides, she knows the only really important thing now is helping Paige get well. And what did Dad say about that? Is she better today?"

Miss Aggie clucked her disapproval over the change of subject, but she answered the question. "He said she's still a little groggy, but she's awake and talking. Doctors think she can come home in a week or so."

Katie poured hot water for her tea from the kettle on the stove. "But she won't be walking, will she?"

"Oh, no. Not for a while. And she has to have some kind of therapy, he said."

"Physical therapy. Exercises, stuff like that. To

make her leg strong again. We'll help with that, too."

Miss Aggie sniffed. "Well, that's all well and good. But you've got your own life to live, too. Your folks won't cotton to your giving all that up. Why don't you run on to school when you've finished your breakfast?"

The toast was cold, so Katie threw it out. She didn't care. She wasn't hungry, anyway. Shaking her head, she said, "No can do. I've got things to do here. I'll go to school tomorrow, I promise." And taking her cup of tea, she went upstairs.

It was hard walking into her bedroom and remembering why Paige wasn't there. If only someone clever would invent a way to go backward in time and erase the bad things, make it as if nothing terrible had ever happened.

She spent most of the morning cleaning Paige's corner of the room. Judy called just before noon to see how Paige was. Katie was just beginning to make some progress and was sitting on the floor staring at a picture she'd found under the bed. It was a picture of Paige with her real mother. They were both laughing. Paige was young, just a tall, skinny seven- or eight-year-old. But there was no mistaking those dark eyes. They were laughing, too, in a way that Katie had never seen.

What was it like to lose your mother when you were only eight years old?

"Can I go visit Paige?" Judy wanted to know.

"I don't think so. Maybe tomorrow."

"That's not fair! *Jake* saw her already, and *I'm* her best friend."

Katie frowned. "Jake? Jake saw her? How do you know?"

"He was here. At school. Looking for you, I think. He said he'd stopped by the hospital and looked in on her. I guess he didn't go in and sit down or anything like that, but he said she waved at him. How come he gets to see her and I don't?"

"Standing outside her room and waving isn't exactly visiting her," Katie replied sourly. "You can see her tomorrow or the day after. I'll let you know, I promise."

Judy had no choice but to accept that. When Katie had hung up, she went back to the room and sat on the floor, staring at dust balls under Paige's bed. Jake had been to the hospital already? She had expected him to wait, to go when *she* went. Was he so worried about Paige that he *couldn't* wait?

I'm being stupid, she scolded herself. Jake is a friend of the family. Why shouldn't he be anxious about Paige? And he had gone to school looking for her. He'd never done that before. Too bad she hadn't been there. It would have been nice to walk through the halls with Jake at her side.

She pulled a tangled web of panty hose, socks, and homework papers out from underneath Paige's bed, and decided that maybe a girl whose mother wasn't around to pester her to clean her room, when she was growing up, shouldn't be blamed for poor housekeeping.

By the time her parents came home for a much-needed break from the hospital, the bedroom was immaculate. Not a wrinkle creased either bedspread, not a speck of dust lurked on any flat surface, and everything Paige owned had been folded, filed, or fit into its proper place. Katie sat on the floor, delighting in the way the late-afternoon sun bounced off the shiny surfaces. She couldn't wait for her mother to see it. Now she would realize that Katie meant to help. The sight of this room might even bring a smile to her face. She liked neat, clean, shiny places.

"That's nice, dear," her mother said from the doorway when Katie persuaded her to take a look. Then, failing to notice the look of utter disappointment on her daughter's face, she added worriedly, "I just hope Paige isn't angry that you touched her things." Then she left to take a shower before dinner.

Katie remained standing in the doorway. She felt as if someone had just slapped her.

"You okay?" Tuck asked as he passed her on his way upstairs. "You look a little green around the edges."

She stared at him. "Oh. Yeah, I'm okay. It's *Paige* who's sick, remember?" And she closed the door in his face.

Shrugging as if to say, "Girls! Go figure!" Tuck went on upstairs.

Dinner that night was a tense affair. The younger girls, happy because their parents were home, were hurt and disappointed by their mother's obvious distraction. Listening for the telephone, she was unable to concentrate on ordinary conversation, and everyone at the table sensed that she was anxious to return to the hospital.

Katie was every bit as withdrawn as her mother, and barely picked at her food, until Bill got her attention by asking when she felt she would be ready for another driving lesson.

Katie gasped in horror. Every sore muscle in her body went rigid. "What? What did you say?"

Her stepfather smiled at her. "I said, when do you want to hit the road again? I brought a rental car home, a small sedan. That will hold us until I can repair the Chevy. So whenever you have the time, I can probably squeeze in half an hour of instruction. And I'm sure Tuck will help, too."

"Oh, really, Bill," Virginia Mae said, her attention caught by the horrified expression on her daughter's face. "It's too soon!"

Her husband shook his head. "You know what they say. It's best to get right back on the horse when you've been thrown."

"Well," Katie said slowly, recovering her composure, "if I had been thrown by a horse, I would get right back on it. Because I've heard that expression, too, and I'm sure it's true. But I wasn't thrown by a horse." Her blue eyes narrowed as her words gathered strength. "I was in an automobile accident. That's not the same thing at all."

Her stepfather shrugged. "Same principle, honey. The longer you wait, the harder it will be to get behind the wheel of a car."

"Good," Katie said calmly, standing up. "Because I'm not going to *get* behind the wheel of a car. Not ever!"

97

"You know you don't mean that, Katie," Bill said.

That irritated her. "I *do* mean it! I do!"

Virginia Mae laid a hand on her husband's arm. "Really, dear," she said, "I think we should respect Katie's wishes in this instance. Not everyone is cut out to be a driver, you know that."

Katie stared at her mother. Instead of feeling supported by having Virginia Mae on her side, she felt betrayed. Could her mother have stated any more clearly that she didn't want her daughter behind the wheel of a car? That she didn't trust her there?

"Right," Katie said in a level voice, her lips white with pain. "Some people shouldn't be allowed behind the wheel of a car."

Virginia Mae looked up, startled. "Oh, Katie, I didn't mean . . ."

Katie waved a hand. "No, it's okay. Really." She took a deep breath and let it out. "Listen, I want to go to the hospital with you tonight. I'll just run up and put something respectable on." A harsh, ragged laugh escaped before she added, "Mustn't let the hospital staff see me looking like this. They'd probably admit me to the psych ward. I'll be right back down. Wait for me." She turned and ran out of the room and up the stairs.

Tuck waited until he heard her bedroom door slam before saying, "It wasn't her fault, Mom." He spoke slowly and deliberately. "It would have happened no matter who was driving." He waited for Virginia Mae to nod acknowledgement, but she didn't.

"Yes, well," she said vaguely, "right now the important thing is for the girls to recover. Everything else will have to go on a back burner for a while."

"Including Katie Summer's driving lessons?" Bill asked quietly.

"Including Katie's driving lessons. As you can see, she's not anxious to resume them herself. Now can we please finish this meal so we can return to the hospital? We've been gone almost two hours. Paige will think we've abandoned her."

"She'll be enjoying the peace and quiet," Bill countered. But he finished his meal, assured the two younger girls that they could visit their sister later in the week, and thanked Tuck for staying home with them so that Miss Aggie could have a well-deserved break. Then he and Virginia waited for Katie.

She looked lovely when she came downstairs. There was no trace of tears on her face, and she had dressed in pale blue trousers and a matching short-sleeved sweater with a white lace collar. Makeup hadn't erased the accident's toll on her face, but she had taken a moment to release her blonde, curly hair from its ponytail and brush it. It hung, loose and full, around her shoulders. "Let's go," she said, her voice free of emotion. "I want to see Paige."

Katie wasn't sure what she expected to find in the hospital room. Paige had almost died and was seriously injured, so she expected that it would be bad. To prepare herself, she practiced deep-breathing exercises during the ride to the hospital. By the time they arrived, she felt prepared. It probably, she told herself as they walked down the corridor, wasn't that bad, anyway.

But it was. It was worse. Her first instinct, which she fought with every ounce of self-control she possessed, was to turn and run. Paige didn't look like Paige. Who *was* this person lying quietly in the white bed, leg in a heavy white cast suspended above the sheets, head wrapped in a thick white turban? The right side of her face was distorted with swelling, changing her jawline, even the set of her mouth. Her dark hair was almost completely hidden, her eyes closed. If I'd come by myself, Katie thought miserably, I'd have been sure I was in the wrong room. She choked back a sob. *I* did this, she thought in anguish. No wonder Mom can't look at me.

Then Paige opened her eyes and said, "Oh, wow! You look worse than *I* do!" Which was so . . . *Paige*, with her way of blurting things out impulsively, that Kate actually laughed.

But it was still hard, watching during the rest of the visit and seeing how little Paige could do for herself. And it was obvious that even with her medication, she was in a great deal of pain. Katie winced every time Paige made the tiniest movement.

It was also obvious that Paige didn't blame Katie in the slightest for the accident. Although talking with a sore jaw was painful, she managed a few well-chosen sentences regarding the nonexistent I.Q. of the other driver. "He must have won his driver's license in a lottery," she fumed.

"Or maybe he's color-blind and can't tell red from green."

Virginia Mae, fussing with Paige's pillow, hushed her. "You're not to get upset. Remember what the doctor said. And please stop talking about the accident. It's too distressing. Poor Katie gets upset every time it's mentioned."

"Poor" Katie stared at her. Her mother was being supportive again, and for the second time that night, it didn't *feel* like support. Am I getting totally paranoid or what, she wondered.

"Katie blames herself," Bill told Paige quietly.

"Well, that's silly! There wasn't anything she could have done."

Virginia Mae tucked in a sheet that needed no tucking. "When you're better," she told Paige, "I want your father to give you some instructions in defensive driving. It's really the only way to drive these days."

There! Katie thought with a sick sense of satisfaction, *that's* why I didn't feel supported a minute ago.

"Well, I'm not going to be driving for a while," Paige said. And wondered silently why Virginia Mae hadn't included Katie Summer in that bit about defensive driving. Something was going on between the two of them, and Paige had no idea what it was. Funny, she thought, looking from mother to daughter, the idea of trouble between the two of them doesn't make me the least bit happy. Isn't *that* a surprise? They had enough problems right at the moment without the added burden of a personal problem between family members.

101

As the family prepared to leave, Katie turned to Paige and said, "I'll come and visit you every day after school."

Paige looked surprised. "Every day? What for? And what about swim practice?"

Katie shrugged. "Don't worry about it. What can I bring for you when I come? Magazines? Books?"

Paige managed a lop-sided grin. "Ben. You can bring me Ben. But you don't have to come every day, Katie."

Yes. I do, Katie thought as they finally managed to drag Virginia Mae out of the room. I do need to come every day.

That's the least I can do.

CHAPTER 11

Jake was waiting on the front porch when they got home. Katie didn't feel like talking, but he persuaded her to walk to the park. It would have seemed pleasant if Katie had been in a better mood.

"So how's Paige?" he asked as they settled on an empty bench under a huge old oak tree, nearly stripped of its leaves.

"Don't you *know*?" She was sorry the minute she'd said it. But it had been a really rotten day. And where had he been? Well, he'd been at the hospital, that much she knew.

He looked over at her. "If I knew, I wouldn't ask. What's *with* you?"

I was in a car wreck, she wanted to say, and my mother's mad at me even though she won't admit it, and my sister's in the hospital because of me, and my father wants me to drive again, and I can't because I know that the minute I get behind the wheel, I'll hear what I hear in my dreams: the sound of Paige screaming.

She didn't say any of that. "I'm just tired," she said instead. "I'm sorry. I guess I was just surprised that you went to the hospital alone instead of waiting for me."

"Katie," taking her arm, he gently pulled her around to face him. "I was down by the hospital on an errand. I wanted to see how she was, that's all. Okay?"

Katie felt very small and very childish. "Sure. We'll go together to visit her some other time."

"So, back to my original question. How was she tonight?"

"Okay, I guess. She looks terrible, but I guess that makes sense."

"You don't look so hot yourself. You feeling okay?"

She was feeling absolutely awful. But after seeing the shape Paige was in, she wasn't going to complain. "She's going to go crazy cooped up in that hospital room," she said, ignoring his question. "We'll all have to keep her entertained until she gets out."

"I'll do what I can. I'm not that busy these days. I can probably take some afternoon time when everyone else is at work or in school and drop in on her then."

Katie tried to ignore the stab of jealousy that statement sent through her. The two of them alone? "That would be nice. I'm sure Paige would be glad to see you." Remembering again that Paige had once wanted Jake for herself, Katie swallowed hard. "Actually," she said, forcing a laugh, "in a day or two, she'll probably be glad to see anyone. I don't think she's going to be a super-terrific patient."

Jake echoed her laugh. "I think that's probably one of the major understatements of all time. She had the flu last year, just for a few days, and the whole family almost went bananas. Miss Aggie said it was like having a caged tiger in the house."

Katie didn't laugh. Wasn't Paige like a caged tiger most of the time? She certainly had her claws out often enough!

"Now," he said, settling back against the bench with his arm around her shoulders, "let's not talk about Paige anymore. We're probably not going to see that much of each other with everyone concentrating on Paige's recovery, so let's not waste the time we have."

He bent to kiss her and she kissed him back, so glad to have someone hold her for a while that she leaned against his chest with a sigh. But during what became a very thorough, satisfactory kiss, her mind was asking, What does Paige's recovery have to do with us being together? I don't like the sound of that. Not one little bit.

But that sort of negative thinking lasted only a brief moment. Then she shoved Paige out of her mind and turned her complete attention to Jake.

Paige, lying dutifully quiet in her hospital bed, hadn't yet reached the point where she felt imprisoned. She drifted in and out of sleep, trying to find a comfortable position. There didn't seem to be one. Paige had no way of knowing it, but her dreams were almost identical to Katie's. The difference was that Paige thought the ear-splitting scream that repeatedly awakened her was Katie's. It wasn't. It was her own.

As her condition slowly began to improve, her room began filling with visitors. Katie, true to her word, arrived every afternoon armed with a book or magazine and the latest school gossip. Judy came, five seconds after Virginia Mae gave her the okay, and Ben came every day, often with Katie.

And that was the hardest thing of all for Paige. It was bad enough watching Katie walk in on two good legs. The bruises on her face were fading and her skin had regained most of its healthy peach glow. Seeing Ben at her side just made it so much worse for Paige. When they explained that since they were both leaving school at the same time for the same destination, it made sense for Katie to grab a ride on Ben's bike, Paige nodded. Of course it made sense. So what? The point was, Katie was out riding around with Ben while certain other people, who *should* have been on the mini-bike, were stuck in a stupid hospital bed! And even if she weren't imprisoned, she certainly couldn't sit behind Ben on his bike. Where would she put this lump of cement they called a cast, this thing she used to call her leg?

Still, things didn't seem as bad when the room was full of people. Virginia Mae was shocked the first time she returned from a coffee break to find them all convulsed in giggles.

"Oh, Mom, relax!" Paige gasped as her step-mother, frowning, hurried to her side. "I don't laugh with my leg!"

106

Although Paige would have bitten her tongue in half rather than say so, her stepmother's constant presence was getting on her nerves. Her pillow couldn't possibly need that much fluffing. And Virginia Mae was so serious. No giggles there. She had tried to talk her stepmother into easing up, returning to her work at the museum, or spending more time at home, but Virginia Mae stood firm. She was always there. Paige felt she should have been grateful, and most of the time she was. But there were those times, like when she had company or wanted to watch something silly on television, or just cry with frustration, or be alone with Ben, when she wished Virginia Mae would take longer coffee breaks.

Oblivious to those feelings in Paige, Katie watched wistfully as Virginia Mae bustled about the room, adjusting, straightening, taking charge. It seemed to Katie that her mother had become a part of the room, as if she now had no other life outside this place.

"I think it's time for everyone to leave," Virginia Mae announced to groans all around. "Things are getting just a bit rowdy in here and Paige must not get overtired. She needs her rest."

"I'm not tired," Paige announced staunchly. She had hoped for a few moments alone with Ben. She knew how busy he was, what with homework and newspaper work, yet he found the time to come here. What good did that do if she had to share him with a crowd? And even if the crowd left, there would still be Virginia Mae.

"That's okay," Ben said, getting up. "I've gotta run, anyway."

107

Paige knew he wouldn't kiss her good-bye. Not with an audience. Not Ben. He kept his demonstrations of affection to a minimum, and he kept them private. Was she *ever* going to have a normal life again?

Not, she decided grimly, if Virginia Mae has anything to say about it. "Out, out, everyone, out now!" her stepmother ordered. "You've all overstayed your welcome."

Easy for *you* to say, Paige thought. But she knew it would be futile to argue. She watched with narrowed eyes as Ben helped Katie with her jacket. Why couldn't Katie put on her own jacket? *She* wasn't lying in a hospital bed.

"If you see Jake, Katie," she said pointedly, "tell him hi for me." She expected a guilty flush in return and got instead a calm, "Oh, sure, Paige, I will. See you tomorrow after school."

The room seemed very empty when they had all gone. "What's Katie doing about swim practice?" Paige asked her stepmother. "I mean, she's here every day. Did she quit the team?"

Virginia Mae stopped pouring ice water into Paige's cup. "Oh. My goodness, I don't know. I hadn't even thought about it. That *is* strange, isn't it? I'll have to ask Katie about that."

And she meant to. While she appreciated the break Katie's arrival at the hospital gave her, swim team was important. She couldn't be permitted to ignore practice.

Paige seemed to be restless after everyone left, and Virginia Mae decided to stay and eat dinner with her. "If I'm not here, I know you won't swallow a bite!" she told Paige. "And you really must build up your strength." Then she decided she might just as well stay until visiting hours were over that evening, since Paige's father had a Bar Association meeting. By the time Virginia Mae left a sleeping Paige to go home, Katie had already been in bed and asleep for more than an hour. Looking in on her, Virginia Mae decided the discussion about swim team would have to wait.

Katie had gone to bed early to avoid thinking. During dinner her father had asked her about swim team, revealing quite innocently that Virginia Mae hadn't even mentioned Katie's presence at the hospital every day after school. If she had even once said, "And Katie comes every day," he wouldn't be asking her now how practice was going, would he? Because he'd know she hadn't been going.

Katie had side-stepped the question, so hurt that she didn't trust herself to speak. Her father probably assumed as she excused herself and went upstairs, that she was worn out from practice. She let him think it. Maybe she should have told him that Coach had warned her today, "Miss one more practice and you're out, Guthrie." She knew what he would say. "Go to practice, Katie. You could always visit Paige in the evening."

Maybe he would be right. Paige had plenty of visitors after school. And Virginia Mae hadn't even noticed that Katie was there. So why, Katie wondered as she crawled into bed, am I jeopardizing something that means as much to me as swim team?

Because, she answered herself as she looked across the room at Paige's empty bed, I have to.

But people at school were beginning to give her a hard time. Her teammates had been arguing with her. "Paige knows how crucial practice is," Ellie Johnson, a freshman member of the team, said at lunch. "She can't possibly expect you to just skip practice to visit her."

"It's not *Paige*," Katie had insisted. "It's me. It's just something I need to do, that's all. You don't understand how awful it is for her, stuck in a hospital bed all day."

Ellie remained unmoved. "And *you* don't understand what it's like for us when you don't show up. Coach takes it out on *us*."

Her classmates made it clear that she was letting them down. Many of them were quick to point out that if the positions were reversed, Paige wouldn't do it for her. Ben was one of those people. "Katie, I admire your loyalty. But keep in mind that Paige wouldn't give up her newspaper work for you."

That surprised her, coming from Ben. "*You* visit her every afternoon," she'd replied as they walked down the second-floor hall after their last period.

"My work on the newspaper lets me be pretty flexible. I can come back later in the day and finish. You can't do that. Coach isn't going to change practice times just for you. Besides, I have a great staff to help me. They can carry some of the load." He'd laughed, then. "I guess that makes me dispensable. But not you. You're one of a kind on that team, Katie, and you know it. The school's going to lose its standing without you."

Katie, lying in bed, thought about Ben's remarks. She had a strong conviction that he was right. Not that she was one of a kind. She probably wasn't. Coach could find someone to take her place. But that would take time, which meant Ben was probably right about the school losing its standing. Because of her. As if she didn't have enough guilt to deal with already.

She ran into him in the hall first thing the following morning. And picked up the discussion where they had left it. "I don't think," she said forcefully, "that you should do something for someone only on the basis of whether or not that person would do the same for you."

"Agreed," Ben said calmly. "But in this case, other people need you as much or maybe more than Paige does." He laughed as they made their way down the stairs. "Anyway, if you're going to be hanging around all the time, when am I going to see Paige alone?"

This time she replied with a laugh of her own. "Okay, okay! You win. I hadn't realized I was being such a nuisance at the hospital. I'll *go* to practice. But," she added with a wry grin, "don't hope for too much at the hospital. I'm not the only one who visits Paige. And even if you get rid of the crowd, there is," she drew the words out dramatically, "still . . . my . . . mother! You'd need a crackerjack S.W.A.T. team to drag *her* away from Paige's bedside."

If Ben heard the slight note of bitterness in her

voice, he ignored it. He chose instead to push her toward the gym door and wave good-bye.

Watching his thin, slightly stooped figure walk away, she decided Paige was, in spite of the accident, a very lucky girl.

Then she went to swim practice.

CHAPTER 12

Annoyed because of her recent absences, Katie's swim coach kept her late, working her every second. By the time she finally dragged into the house, dinner was well under way. And her mother was at the table, a sight that eased Katie's exhaustion. Smiling happily, she apologized for involuntarily breaking the household rule about everyone being home in time for the evening meal. Maybe now, she thought as she slid into her chair, we can start having normal family meals again, if Mom is going to stop eating at the hospital with Paige.

Her stepfather must have been thinking along the same lines. "You're forgiven," Bill said, returning her smile and passing her the meat platter. "I've talked your mother into taking her evening meal with us from now on. It's time we got back to our usual routine around here."

So, Katie thought, scooping mashed potatoes

onto her plate, *he* talked her into it. And she doesn't look very happy about it. I guess she'd rather be with Paige. But she refused to let that thought darken her good mood. It had felt so wonderful to be in the water again, to feel strong and capable and in charge, to know she was doing a good job. How could she have considered giving it up?

"I think Paige was disappointed when you didn't show up this afternoon," Virginia Mae said suddenly, catching Katie off-guard. "She was expecting you."

"Well, I . . ." Katie began, but her mother interrupted.

"I realize you have things to do. We all do. But it does seem, in view of Paige's situation, that we could put those other things on hold for a little while, don't you think?"

"If I hadn't gone to swim practice today," Katie said quietly, her eyes on her plate, "I would have been thrown off the team. I didn't think that would make you very happy."

"Of course it wouldn't, kitten," Bill injected, frowning in his wife's direction. "Swim team is very important. Paige understands that."

"I'm sure," Virginia Mae, undaunted by her husband's frown, persisted, "that if you explained the situation to your coach, he would make allowances."

"He already knows, Mother. Everyone at school knows. It doesn't make any difference. I still have to go to practice."

Tuck came to her rescue. "Paige doesn't need

Katie there, anyway, Mom. Judy comes every day and so does Ben. And Jake's been coming a lot."

Katie's head jerked up. A lot? Jake had been visiting Paige a lot?

"He comes in the afternoon while school is still in session," Tuck explained, understanding the expression on her face. He'd been trying to help Katie out, but right now she looked worse than she had before he'd opened his big mouth. "I guess he figures that's when nobody else can come, so he might as well. I mean," he finished lamely, "his work schedule is pretty flexible."

As if he'd never said a word, Virginia Mae continued, "I think you can find time for your sister, Katie," destroying the very last shred of Katie's good mood. "After all — "

Katie jumped up, her blue eyes filling with angry tears. "Go ahead!" she cried. "Say it! Just say it! I know what you're thinking. You're thinking, After all, if it weren't for Katie Summer, Paige wouldn't *be* in the hospital. Why don't you just *say* it?"

A shocked Virginia gasped, "Katie!" Megan and Mary Emily exchanged frightened glances, Tuck shook his head in disgust at yet another family meal ruined, and Bill protested, "Katie, your mother isn't thinking any such thing!" Turning to his wife, he urged, "*Tell* her!"

"I most certainly wa*s not* thinking that," Virginia Mae, her face white and strained, said. "I was about to say, After all, it gets very lonely in a hospital room."

Katie wasn't buying. "Not for Paige," she said

harshly. "How could Paige possibly be lonely? She's got *you* — every single second of every single day, she's got you."

Virginia Mae flinched. "I'm here now."

"Yes," Katie said, pushing her chair away from the table, "but you'd rather be there, with her. It's written all over your face. I'll bet you had an absolute fit when Bill insisted you come home and spend some time with the rest of us."

The glance Katie's parents exchanged told her she'd scored a bull's-eye. "Well, as far as I'm concerned," she continued, "you can stay at the hospital all day and all night if you want to."

Megan and Mary Emily gasped. They had never heard Katie talk to her mother in that tone of voice. And Bill warned, "Katie, take it easy."

She ignored him. "Because even when you *are* here, you'd rather not be. And we can all tell." She took a deep breath and let it out. "I didn't go to the hospital this afternoon and I'm not going tonight, either. I have too much homework, something else I've been ignoring lately." Turning to face her stepfather, she said, "I'm sorry, Dad, about all of this. Please tell Paige I hope she's feeling better. Because I really do." Then she turned and headed for the stairs.

Behind her, she heard her stepfather urge, "Virginia Mae, go and talk to her." And then her mother's reply after a moment's hesitation: "No. Not now. She's too upset and so am I. Besides, we've got to get back to the hospital. Paige will think we're not coming."

Smiling bitterly, Katie went upstairs and into her room.

At the hospital, when Virginia Mae had apologized for the third time for Katie's absence, Paige burst out irritably, "It's *okay*, Mom! So she's got homework. I mean, it's not like we're bosom buddies. We don't have that much to talk about, anyway."

That was certainly true enough, Paige thought to herself. Why was Virginia Mae making such a big deal about Katie's absence? Because, the answer came readily, it's important to her to see us as one big happy family. So the sister who isn't flat on her back in a hospital bed should be eagerly rushing to the side of the sister who *is*. That was Virginia Mae's image of how things should be.

Paige choked back a giggle. The picture of Katie Summer rushing to her side was just too funny. Although she had to admit, Katie had been showing up faithfully. Until today. And Ben had explained that this afternoon when he dropped by. "It was you or swim team. I told her to pick swim team. That's a lot more fun than listening to you complain about your aches and pains." Virginia Mae had gone down to the cafeteria and they were alone.

"I don't complain!" she'd protested, but that crooked grin of his had melted her anger. He was right, anyway. Swim team was important. And she certainly wouldn't have given up the newspaper to visit Katie, if the accident had had different results.

"Relax, Mom," she said, rolling her eyes toward Tuck, who was sitting quietly in a corner.

"Katie has better things to do than sit around a stuffy old hospital room. I'll bet you guys do, too. Why don't you call it a night and head for home?" She was hoping Ben would stop by. "And if you pass Ben coming in when you're on your way out," she warned, "do *not* tell him I'm asleep!"

But her hopes were dashed a moment later when Ben called to say he couldn't make it. Before she could express her disappointment, he said, "Listen, I'm going to have to put you to work. I need some help with copy for the next issue."

"Ben. I'm in the hospital. There is a cast on my leg."

He laughed. "Since when do you write with your leg? C'mon, Paige, you can't just lie around all day. Help me out here, okay? I'll bring the stuff by tomorrow and we'll go over it together." Without waiting for an answer, he told her to sleep tight and hung up.

"Of all the nerve," Paige said, handing her mother the receiver. "He wants me to *work* while I'm in here."

Her mother's mouth dropped open. "Who? Who wants you to work?"

"Ben. He's bringing copy over tomorrow."

"Here? He expects you to do newspaper work here?" Virginia Mae looked genuinely shocked.

Paige didn't want her mother mad at Ben. She back-tracked quickly. "Well, it's just editing."

"I think that's a terrific idea," Bill said heartily. "Why not? You'll be going home soon, but until then it'll keep you busy."

"She doesn't *need* anything to keep her busy," his wife said. "She's recuperating."

Paige hated it when they talked about her in the third person. "Hey, you two, relax! I'm right here, remember? Please don't discuss me as if I were on another planet." She appealed to Tuck for help, signaling him with her eyes that she needed him to run interference for her. But he shook his head and got up and walked out of the room. No help there.

"Tell you what, Mom. I'll just take a look at the stuff Ben's bringing over, okay? And if I'm too tired, I just won't do the copy. But remember, he's short on time because he's spending so much of it here, so fair is fair, right?"

Virginia reluctantly gave in, but Paige had a feeling that when tomorrow and the copy arrived, the discussion might well begin all over again.

When they had gone (finally! Paige thought), she lay restless and uncomfortable in the empty room. She was beginning to realize that the accident had affected more lives than just her own. She might be in the hospital when no one else was, but something unpleasant was going on at home. Judging from the strained look on Virginia Mae's face when she had explained that Katie wasn't coming to the hospital, whatever was wrong had something to do with the two of them. And it probably has something to do with me, too, she thought, since I seem to be all Virginia Mae is focusing on these days. She groaned. Going home wasn't going to be the thrill she'd anticipated if there was trouble there. Maybe she'd just stay where she was.

Even if that had been a serious thought, it lasted only until the next day when Ben brought material for her to edit. Going over the copy with him made her feel normal for the first time since the accident. And it made her anxious to leave the hospital and rejoin the outside world.

"Attagirl!" Ben applauded when she shared that thought. "That's the kind of talk I like to hear." Virginia Mae had reluctantly agreed to get a cup of coffee, and no other visitors had arrived, so they were alone. His voice softened as he moved his chair closer to her bed. "I've missed you." He sounded surprised. "Things are pretty dull without you around."

Paige grinned. She knew it wasn't easy for Ben to say things like that. Moving carefully, she lifted her head to give him a quick kiss of appreciation.

Well, maybe not so quick. It was still in progress when Katie walked in, armed with two magazines and a book, her hair still damp from swim practice.

"Oops, sorry!" she declared, hastily backing away, her cheeks pink with embarrassment.

Ben stopped her. "No problem," he said with a crooked grin. "I've gotta go, anyway. You can take over here." He stood up, motioning for Katie to take his seat. "Your mom will be back in a minute. But, this one here," he glanced down at Paige who was frowning fiercely at her stepsister for interrupting, "has work to do. So see if you can talk your mom into going home and letting Paige work in peace, okay?"

"That won't be easy," Katie replied, sitting down. She couldn't help wishing her mother would follow Ben's example and treat Paige more matter-of-factly, instead of babying her.

"Well, give it a shot, okay? This stuff is important. Catch you later." And he was gone, leaving the two of them alone for the first time since that rainy Sunday afternoon.

It was awkward. Katie made an effort. She handed her stepsister the magazines and book she'd brought. "Maybe I shouldn't have brought these," she said with a grin. "I didn't know Ben was going to be assigning you newspaper work."

Paige barely glanced at the magazines before tossing them aside. The book she handed back to Katie, saying, "I've read this author's stuff before. He's really boring."

Rude, rude, rude! Katie thought angrily, but she swallowed her feelings. Sick people shouldn't be expected to act normally, she reminded herself. But that generous thought was quickly followed by, Who am I kidding? For Paige this *is* normal!

She was saved from further attempts at a one-on-one conversation with her stepsister by the arrival of their mother. Virginia Mae hurried into the room overflowing with apologies for having been gone so long.

Katie wanted to say, It doesn't matter, Mom. Paige has been just fine, even with you out of the room. She can survive without you hovering over her every single second.

And Paige wanted to say, It doesn't matter,

Mom. Ben was here and I'd rather be alone with him than have you standing over us every single second.

Neither of them said one word. They both knew the words would fall on deaf ears.

CHAPTER 13

As Paige became stronger, it became increasingly difficult for Katie Summer to summon up sympathy for her. The hospital crowds gradually thinned, the novelty of visiting having worn off, and Paige gradually became crankier. The magazines and books Katie brought were "boring," the homework assignments she took pains to collect for Paige "a pain," and not once did Katie receive a thank-you for her efforts.

And there was something else. While Paige had once upheld Katie's innocence regarding the accident, as she became crankier, she also became more resentful. And more demanding. As if, Katie thought angrily, I owe her. But she said it wasn't my fault.

The demands and commands increased. "Katie, this water is warm. I need ice." And, "Katie, there are better magazines in the sunroom. Get me a couple of those." And "Katie,

Ben needs this copy right away. You don't mind running back to school with it, do you?"

School was twenty minutes away by bus. But when she said, "Paige, I just *came* from there," her mother sent her a warning look that clearly said, She can't go herself, Katie. Can't you do this for her?

Katie did it. And when a grateful Ben remarked, "You look beat, Katie," she laughed harshly. So she looked beat, did she? Small wonder.

She didn't go back to the hospital, taking the bus home instead. During the ride, she thought of Jake whom she hadn't seen much of lately. Maybe he blames me for Paige's accident, too. After all, he was Paige's friend first. And he *has* been visiting her a lot. Always when I'm not there.

Katie had a queasy feeling in her stomach, one she couldn't blame on bus fumes. Jake spending all that time alone with Paige, was that sympathy? Or something stronger? Something that had been there all along but hadn't been recognized by Jake until Paige almost died?

Katie sank back in her seat, sighing deeply. Had she ever been this tired in her entire life? Although she was taking pains to collect and deliver Paige's school assignments, she never seemed to have time or energy for her own schoolwork. With her mother still spending evenings at the hospital, Miss Aggie needed a certain amount of help at home, and the two younger girls needed a certain amount of comforting. Then there was swim practice and meets and visiting Paige. She seldom saw her own friends anymore; there was no time for socializing. I can't remember, she thought dismally as the bus stopped at the corner, what it feels like to just go out and have a good time.

She felt very, very old. Laughing softly to herself as she got off the bus, she thought it was really ironic that Jake's objection to their relationship was that she was too young for him. Now that she felt at least a thousand years old, where was he?

In her room, she decided that she wasn't all that sure Paige's return home would be as big a relief as she had once thought. True, there'd be no more hospital visits, and her mother would no longer be absent so much. But, glancing around the clean, peaceful room she'd had all to herself lately, she found it hard to get excited about Paige's impending discharge from the hospital.

Claiming honestly that she had too much homework, she begged off the evening hospital visit that night. But the following evening she didn't even try, knowing that two nights in a row would be too much for Virginia Mae. She'd get *that* look.

As if to prove that she was enthusiastic about this visit, Katie hurried down the hall ahead of her parents when they reached the hospital. The truth was, she always rushed through an unpleasant task, to get it out of the way faster. But she was fairly sure her parents weren't interpreting her eagerness correctly.

She pushed open the door to Paige's room. And found her stepsister in the arms of Jake Carson.

At first, Katie assumed the arms belonged to Ben. A natural assumption, she told herself later with some bitterness. After all, Paige was dating Ben, not Jake.

But as she called out, "Hi, guys!" several things quickly corrected the assumption that Ben Collins was hugging her stepsister. The first was the way they jumped apart. The second was the guilty look on Paige's face as they jumped apart. And the third was that the face turning toward Katie was not thin and bespectacled. It was strong-jawed, full-lipped, and incredibly handsome. It was Jake Carson.

"Oh, excuse me," Katie Summer stammered. Hadn't she played this scene out before? But the boy in that scene had been a different boy. That boy *had* been Ben and seeing him with Paige hadn't sent a knife through her heart. No wonder Jake had been visiting Paige so often. There were obviously fringe benefits.

"Hi, Sweetie!" Virginia Mae called brightly to Paige, bypassing Katie and advancing straight to Paige's bedside. She failed to notice the stricken look on Katie's face, or the guilty one on Paige's. Katie's father, entering behind his wife, noticed both expressions.

"What's going on?" he asked Katie, who was still frozen just inside the doorway.

"Nothing," she said quickly. "But I'm not feeling too well. Can I just go out in the hall for a minute?"

Bill nodded. He threw an accusing glance in Paige's direction. Paige knew that her father didn't for one second believe Katie had suddenly become ill, but he couldn't possibly know what had taken place. And I'm not about to tell him. Paige thought, making an effort to look as innocent as possible. And wasn't it just like Katie to jump to conclusions like that?

"I'll come with you," Jake offered, standing up.

"No!" Katie cried sharply. Bill arched his eyebrows in suspicion. She didn't *sound* sick. She sounded . . . angry. What now?

"I mean," Katie added, "I'd really rather be alone. You stay here. With Paige." And she turned and left the room.

"I'm going, too," Jake announced. He knew perfectly well why Katie wasn't feeling well, and he wasn't content to leave it at that.

"Really, Jake," Paige said plaintively, "she said she wanted to be alone."

"Yeah, but she didn't mean it. See you later. Take it easy, okay?" Saying good-bye to Paige's confused parents, he hurried after Katie.

He found her sitting on a bench in the hall. Pale-faced and tight-lipped, she was a study in anger and hurt. But, he thought as he sat down, even in anger she's beautiful.

Knowing he had caused the hurt put him on the defensive. "Don't you want to know what happened?" he asked, facing her.

She refused to look at him, staring straight ahead at the door to Paige's room. "I *know* what happened. I have eyes." She was so proud of herself for not giving in to tears.

"You have gorgeous eyes. But you didn't see what you think you saw."

She crossed her legs and began swinging one

booted foot impatiently. As angry as she was with him, she was glad she'd worn the pale blue sweater and skirt. She would look good when she told him to leave. "Oh, really? Well, maybe I need to get my eyes checked."

Her calmness infuriated him. "What you saw," he bit off the words one at a time, "was a friend comforting another friend. And that's *all* you saw."

Katie hooted. "Right! Anyone could see that. Why, my goodness, I comfort my male friends at school in just that way every single day."

Jake reached out and grabbed her arm. "Look at me, Katie! I *said*, look at me!"

She turned her head angrily — away from him.

"Your friends at school aren't in the hospital. They're not bored and they don't feel like the rest of the world has left them behind. They're not scared to death that they'll never live a full life again. That's what happens to people when they're in the hospital. It's not a normal way to live and so they don't feel normal and it's very scary."

She bit her lower lip.

"I put my arms around her because she was feeling all of those things, because there was no one else there to comfort her, and because I'm her friend. Don't turn it into something it wasn't." He took Katie's chin in one hand and forced her to meet his gaze. "What I *didn't* do was this." He kissed Katie, firmly, with a mixture of love and anger that should have left no doubt in her mind about his feelings for her.

Ordinarily, it would have done just that. But Katie's emotional antennae had been so overloaded for so long, they weren't receiving with their usual accuracy. She pulled away. Chin still high, she said in a shaky voice, "I'm sorry. I shouldn't have made such a fuss. You certainly have a right to put your arms around anyone you choose. Now, if you'll excuse me, I have to get back inside." She stood up, brushing at her skirt as if it could somehow have become dusty there in the antiseptic corridor. Anything to avoid looking at him. "If Paige is as upset as you say, she needs her family around her."

Jake knew that tone of voice well. That was her I'm-hurt-but-I-have-my-pride voice. He hated it when she did that. "There is nothing between Paige and me except friendship," he said flatly.

"See you later." Head high, boot heels clicking on the white tiles, she walked to Paige's room and disappeared inside.

Jake went home.

Maybe, Katie thought as she approached Paige's bed, maybe all Jake felt *was* friendship. Maybe he was telling the truth about that. But he didn't realize that Paige had felt a lot more than that for a long time, until Ben came along. And maybe even now, for all anyone knew. Maybe Paige had just settled for Ben because she couldn't have Jake.

Or could she?

"Dad says you're coming home pretty soon," Katie said stiffly, sitting in the chair vacated earlier by Jake and ignoring the questioning looks

129

of her parents. "Everyone's excited about that." It couldn't be really wrong to lie to sick people, could it?

"Everyone?" Paige grinned. "You must have loved having the room all to yourself." Her eyes narrowed. "You didn't touch any of my stuff, did you? In a cleaning frenzy, for instance?"

Katie felt herself flushing. How had Paige guessed?

Virginia Mae answered for her. "She just straightened a few things, that's all. The room looks very nice. Besides, you won't be able to sleep up there for a while."

Katie heaved a sigh of relief.

Paige groaned. "Why not?"

"The stairs. You can't negotiate those on crutches. We're going to fix up a nice bed for you in the playroom, just for a little while."

"She should feel right at home there," Katie said, remembering Paige in Jake's arms. She forced a small laugh. "That's where she goes to get away from me."

Ignoring that, Virginia Mae added, "And having you downstairs will make it easier on everyone when we begin helping you with your physical therapy. And we'll *all* be helping." Her eyes went to Katie.

Katie shrugged. "Sure. I'd love to help." At that moment, the thought of turning Paige into a pretzel was enormously appealing. Maybe there was justice in the world, after all.

Then she remembered Jake's words about how bad Paige had been feeling, and she was ashamed. While Virginia Mae described the redecorating that would take place in the playroom, Katie studied her stepsister. She doesn't *look* miserable, she thought. The thick turban on her head had been replaced by a smaller bandage across her forehead, and her leg was no longer in traction.

But Jake hadn't said she was *just* in pain. Hadn't he said something about how she felt abnormal? Katie swallowed a laugh. Well, she *is* abnormal: abnormally rude, abnormally hostile, abnormally arrogant. . . .

But that wasn't what Jake had meant. He had said that being in the hospital made Paige feel like she was no longer part of the real world. Was that true? She supposed it could be. Life was going on outside the way it always did, but Paige was removed from all of it. Maybe she was scared that she'd never be a part of it again.

Then why doesn't she say so? She could have talked to me, Katie told herself, even as she realized that Paige would never do that. Never!

Well, she could have told Virginia Mae then, or Bill, or even Tuck. They might have understood.

What she didn't have to do, Katie decided, standing up and walking over to the window, was throw herself into Jake Carson's arms.

And I don't think I feel like forgiving her for that.

By the time they left the hospital that night, Katie had decided that she wouldn't forgive Paige until Virginia Mae forgave *her* for putting Paige in the hospital. Fair was fair, after all.

CHAPTER 14

When Paige came home from the hospital, the whole family made every effort to create a pleasant homecoming. While Bill and Tuck went to pick up the discharged patient, Katie willingly aided Virginia in her hunt for every last speck of dust. Megan and Mary Emily spent hours designing a huge banner to hang over the front door. It read, in bright red Magic Marker, WELCOME HOME, PAIGE. When it had been hung, the four of them busied themselves turning the playroom into an attractive, comfortable room that Megan dubbed "the recovery room." They had borrowed the extra single bed from Tuck's room and decorated it with a beautiful star-patterned red and white quilt. Megan and Mary Emily had painted several pictures to hang on the paneled walls. Virginia Mae placed a small end table by the bed on which she placed a lamp, several books, some magazines, and a thermos filled with cold water. When the room was ready, Virginia Mae stood back, clasped her hands together, and said with satisfaction, "There! I declare, it looks very pretty. Paige will be so pleased."

Well, she should be, Katie thought wearily. Foreign dignitaries visiting the White House don't get this great a reception!

If Paige was pleased, she didn't show it. Katie could see that Virginia Mae was disappointed. But she could also see that the trip home had exhausted Paige. Her face looked as if it had been bleached and the corners of her mouth were pinched with pain. They wasted no time getting her into bed. Her cast had been removed early that morning, but the leg was still thickly bandaged.

"Tomorrow," Virginia Mae said, "we begin physical therapy. But you can rest today."

Taking her at her word, Paige was asleep in minutes.

She awoke later that day, just in time to, as Virginia Mae put it, "receive guests." Judy arrived first, followed closely by Ben, and then Jake. Katie, watching them all congregate in the small playroom, decided the only differences between the hospital room and the playroom were the colorful quilt and a lack of nurses. As in taking-care-of-patient nurses. Paige was demanding . . . mostly of Katie. I am *not*, Katie thought as she went to the kitchen for the fourth time to fetch ice, a waitress. Hasn't anyone noticed that I am not wearing a little white apron or carrying an order pad? Not only that, Jake had barely acknowledged her existence. He came in, said hello, and headed straight for the playroom.

Katie gave the refrigerator door a good kick as she closed it. So he was going to play *that* game, was he? Well, she could play it, too. She would pretend Jake Carson was a figment of her imagination. He didn't exist. As of this moment, he fell into the same category as leprechauns, the tooth fairy, and the pot of gold at rainbow's end.

But it wasn't easy. At one point, she had to bite her tongue to keep from saying sarcastically, "Jake, for someone who intends to study law, you're sure acting a lot like a doctor!" He kept hovering over Paige, asking if he could get her anything. But when she said yes, which was fairly often, instead of getting it himself, he'd say casually, "Katie, Paige needs something good to drink." The third time he sent her on an errand for Paige, she had to clench her fists to keep from dumping the pitcher of lemonade on his handsome head. Ben wasn't giving her orders. He was talking to Paige, telling her what was going on at the newspaper. What was Jake trying to prove? That she had to make up for what she'd done to Paige, by waiting on her hand and foot? Had he decided she *was* responsible for the accident? Then why didn't he just come right out and say so, instead of ordering her around as if she were his and Paige's servant?

As annoyed as she was with him, she was still disappointed when he left with Judy and Ben. He hadn't said a word to her about going out that night. It seemed forever since they'd spent any time together alone.

When she returned to the playroom after letting the guests out, Paige stunned her by saying casually, "Could you please run upstairs and get my red sweater? It's in my sweater drawer, I think." She thought for a minute. "Or maybe it's on the floor of my closet, behind my shoes. I'm not sure. But everyone's coming back after dinner and I want to ditch these stupid pajamas. There's no reason why I can't wear regular clothes."

"Everyone?" Katie, poised in the doorway, frowned. "Jake, too?"

Paige looked smug. "Jake, too."

Katie thought longingly of ice cubes in the bed or pancake syrup in the hair. She quickly dismissed those ideas as being too juvenile, too summer-campish. But it was tempting.

"Katie, on your way back in here, could you get me something to drink?"

Katie looked pointedly at the wooden crutches Megan had painted buttercup yellow and dotted with glued-on sequins. They were perched beside Paige's bed. "Dad says you're supposed to use those. I don't mind getting things for you, but he said you've been lying in bed too long. Shouldn't you try them?"

Paige's face crumpled. "Oh, Katie, if you knew how much it hurts. . . ."

"Okay, okay! I'll fetch and carry! Relax!"

But when she brought the can of juice, Paige said, "Oh, Katie, not *that* kind! I hate that kind! And are there any chips? I'm starved."

Probably from all that exercise you've been getting, Katie thought nastily. But she turned on her heel and went to fetch the "right" kind of drink. In the kitchen, Virginia Mae looked up as Katie opened the refrigerator door. "I really appreciate all you're doing for Paige," she said. "I'm sure she does, too."

Oh, sure, Katie thought as she switched juice cans. I can see the undying gratitude oozing out of Paige's every pore.

Her mother's attitude toward her had changed, though. Since Paige's arrival that morning, Virginia Mae had been friendlier, more relaxed, and had even put her arm around Katie's shoulders once or twice. Maybe now that the worst was over, Katie thought as she returned to the playroom, they could mend the hole in their relationship. That would be a relief.

But there was another problem. On her way back to Paige's room, her stepfather stopped her in the hall. "Well, Katie," he said in a cheerful voice, "now that Paige is home, maybe life in this house will get back to normal, hmm?"

She nodded wearily. "Whatever *that* was."

He laughed. "Well, part of the routine was your driving lessons, remember?"

Katie's face went dead-white and she slumped against the wall. "No, I can't," she whispered. "Don't make me!"

Alarmed by her reaction, Bill said, "Hey, hey, hey! Take it easy. I didn't mean right this minute!"

She looked up at him, hope in her face. Was he going to let her off the hook?

His next words dashed that hope. "But honey, you can't let this one accident stop you. You need to get that license. You'd be dependent upon other people for the rest of your life without a driver's license, and you'd hate that."

Not as much as I'd hate getting behind the wheel of a car, she answered silently. "I live in a city," she said aloud, "with mass transit all over the place. That would give me my independence."

"Katie, you don't know what the future holds. You may not always live in a city." But he hadn't meant to upset her, and the conversation wasn't going anywhere, he could see that. The matter would just have to wait. "You run along. We'll talk about it later. I've got some briefs to go over, then I'll be in to see Paige."

She "ran along." If I have to, she vowed, I will burn that stupid learner's permit.

Jake, Ben, and Judy arrived after dinner. And later, Tuck brought Jennifer Bailey in for a visit. Katie caught the look of disappointment on Judy's face when Tuck walked in with Jennifer on his arm, and a smile on his face, and thought, Oh. I didn't know. I wonder if Paige knows. Poor Judy. Tuck has worked so hard to get Jennifer's attention, he's probably never even noticed Judy.

Personally, she thought as she made her way to the kitchen once again, I think he'd be better off with Judy. She's so nice. And Jennifer keeps bouncing like a Ping-Pong ball from our star quarterback to Tuck and back to Ed Thomas again. Tuck must be very confused.

Aren't we all? she asked herself, and she

pulled open the refrigerator door for what seemed like the thousandth time that day.

Walking back to the playroom, tray in hand, she wondered if Jake would tear himself away from Paige long enough to talk to her. Without giving her an order.

Not only did Jake not talk to her, he continued to act as if she weren't on the same planet. When he suggested a game of Scruples and didn't invite her to play, Katie excused herself and went up to her room, thinking, Let them get their own drinks!

Almost, but not quite, wishing that Paige had stayed in the hospital, Katie settled down to several hours of overdue homework. But Jake's laughter filtering up from downstairs ruined her concentration. Eventually, she gave up and went to bed, feeling lost and lonely.

She was awakened the following morning by a blood-curdling scream of pain. She thought at first it had been the nightmare again. But she was awake now, and the screaming continued. The terrible sound echoed throughout the house. Jumping up and tossing on her robe, Katie raced downstairs to the playroom.

Paige was lying in bed, her face and hair soaked with tears, both hands clutching her bandaged leg. Virginia Mae stood by the bed, looking stricken. Her husband was at her side, trying to calm her down. The rest of the family and Miss Aggie stood just inside the playroom, all looking shocked and worried.

"What's going on?" Katie cried.

Virginia Mae took a deep breath. "Her exercises," she said shakily. "They're . . . very pain-ful."

"I . . . can't . . . do . . . this!" Paige gasped. "I can't! It's too soon! It hurts too much!"

Every nasty thought she'd ever had about Paige came back to haunt Katie, consuming her with guilt. She couldn't bear the look on her step-sister's face.

"Honey," Bill said to Paige, "your mom and I don't want to hurt you, you know that." He took one of her hands and held it in both of his. "But the doctors made it clear that if you're ever to have full use of that leg again, you must do these exercises."

"No! No, I won't!"

Virginia Mae moved closer to the bed. "Paige, it's because this is the first time. You haven't used that leg since the accident."

And Bill added, "If you don't do the exercises, the muscles will atrophy. You don't want that, Paige."

"I don't want *this*," Paige cried, fresh tears welling up in her eyes. "I don't want *any* of it!" The shock of encountering pain again when she had thought life would become easier, was too much for her. All of her anger and fear and frus-tration came spilling out. "I want to be out of this bed! I want to get these bandages off! I want to be normal again, like everyone else!" Ex-hausted she fell back upon the pillow, sobbing wildly. "It's not fair. It's not fair!" she whispered.

Katie looked at her mother. There was no ac-cusation in Virginia Mae's eyes, but that didn't help. Because Paige was right. It really wasn't fair. *I* should be in that bed, Katie thought, not her.

"I know it's not fair, honey," Bill said. "But you just said you want to be normal again. That's what the therapy is for, Paige."

"Please, Bill," his wife said softly, tugging on his sleeve. "Let's let it go for today. You can see she's in no shape to continue."

"No," he said firmly. "And please don't make me the heavy here. She has to do this. You know that, and I think Paige does, too."

Paige did. She wanted, with everything in her, to refuse to do the exercises. But even more than that, she wanted to be healthy again. And the way there included the therapy.

"Okay, okay," she whispered, wiping her face with the edge of the sheet. "Give me a minute. Then you can start torturing me again."

"I can't," Virginia Mae said with some difficulty. "I just can't. I'm sorry. Bill? You'll have to do it."

His face was grim, but he nodded.

"No," Katie said, moving into the room. "I'll do it."

Everyone stared at her.

"Show me what to do and I'll do it. I promise I'll be very gentle."

No one said a word.

Slowly it dawned on Katie what they were all thinking. She felt her cheeks grow hot. "You don't really think I'd *hurt* her, do you?" she asked. "No one thinks that, do they?"

"No, no, of course not," Virginia Mae said hastily. And it seemed to Katie that her words were sincere. "And if you're sure you're up to it, I would be grateful if you'd help. I'm sure Paige would be, too."

Katie heaved a sigh of relief. Fetching and carrying for Paige hadn't repaired the rift between herself and her mother, not totally. Maybe helping Paige with her therapy would do that.

"Paige?" She turned toward her stepsister. "That okay with you? You trust me to take it easy on your bones?"

Deciding quickly that Katie would be an easier taskmaster than her father, Paige nodded. "Why not?" she said.

CHAPTER 15

True to her word, Katie Summer followed
through in aiding Paige with her exercises with
diligence and gentleness. The goal Paige had set
for herself was negotiating the stairs. Feelings in
the family about the attainment of that goal were
varied. Paige considered it a challenge and viewed
it as a giant step toward recovery. Her parents
and all siblings but one looked forward to it with
increasing anticipation as a restless, impatient
Paige made life in the playroom more and more
difficult. Katie Summer, even as she worked to
help her stepsister recover full use of the injured
leg, dreaded the moment when Paige resumed
occupancy of their shared bedroom. How she
loved the privacy she enjoyed now! Time spent
downstairs since Paige's return home had become full of tension and physical demands. Time
spent upstairs was peaceful and relaxing. All of
that would change the moment Paige conquered

weak muscles and damaged tissue and successfully made her uphill climb.

But Katie had to admit, when the moment came, that it was an exciting, triumphant time for her stepsister. After an inch-by-inch struggle, Paige stood at the top of the stairs, waving one crutch in the air. Virginia Mae, at the foot of the stairs, cried quietly, while Megan, Mary Emily, and Tuck cheered and clapped. And Katie could see that Bill was having trouble holding back tears of his own.

She felt mean and selfish for wanting this moment of triumph for Paige to wait just a while longer.

That was a feeling that quickly disappeared as their bedroom became Grand Central Station for visitors, with people arriving and departing as often as trains. The peace and quiet she had enjoyed became a thing of the past. With Paige upstairs, Katie and her family made so many trips up and down they all began to feel, as Tuck put it, "like elevators." But Katie was the one who shared the room, and so most of the burden fell to her. Between homework and swim practice (neither of which she felt were under control), and meeting Paige's almost-constant demands, she felt fragmented.

In spite of the fact that Katie was now sharing a room again, she felt very alone. Her parents had no time for her, especially her mother, who had returned to her duties as museum docent for a few hours two days a week. Jake had no time for her. And I, Katie thought unhappily as she approached the dinner table several days after Paige had ascended the stairs, I have no time for *any-one*. Sara and Diane and Lisa and everyone else at school probably think I've become totally anti-social!

At least Paige was eating her evening meal at the table now, which saved Katie one "elevator" trip. Wearing pajamas and robe because slipping into jeans had proved to be too difficult, Paige, her dark hair in a ponytail, chattered away about the TV shows she'd watched that day. She ended her remarks with, "I just think it's so unfair that younger drivers have to pay higher insurance rates."

Katie's arm stopped taking a forkful of spaghetti toward her mouth. Uh-oh, she thought, feeling her stepfather's eyes on her face. Of all the subjects for Paige to introduce!

"Katie Summer," Bill said, justifying her fear, "I think it's time we got back to your driving lessons, don't you?"

Darn Paige's big mouth! Katie shot her a look that clearly said, Why don't you zip it up? before answering Bill. "No, not really," she said in a deliberately calm voice. "I don't have time just now." She didn't want another scene. No point in ruining a perfectly good meal although she herself wasn't the slightest bit hungry.

"We'll find the time," he said just as calmly. Virginia Mae signaled a warning with her eyes, which he ignored. "Paige is used to the physical therapy now, so maybe Virginia Mae can help her while you and I take to the road."

Katie's lower lip began to tremble. Did he have

to do this now? In front of the entire family? She would *not* cry in front of Paige!

"And you're not eating anything," Bill continued. "You haven't been eating enough lately," gesturing toward her plate. "Is anything wrong?"

She lifted her head to stare at him. Was he serious? Didn't he know anything about her life? Was he, like her mother, so wrapped up in Paige's recovery that he was blind to everything else?

Hurt, tired, and lonely, Katie Summer laughed. And once she started laughing, she couldn't stop. With uncertain, nervous half-smiles on their faces, because they didn't know what to do, her family watched as peal after peal of laughter escaped Katie's lips.

She put her hands over her mouth, but that didn't help. "Is anything *wrong?*" she managed to gasp, "Is anything wrong?" More uncontrollable giggles, then, "What could possibly be wrong?"

"Katie, stop it!" Bill ordered, understanding what was happening.

She looked at him, her eyes filling with tears. "I can't," she whispered. "I can't stop it. I have to be excused. Please?"

He nodded. When she had pushed away from the table, he turned to his wife, awaiting her reaction. Virginia Mae said nothing, and Katie left the room.

"Don't you think you'd better go talk to her?" Bill asked Katie's mother.

Virginia Mae hesitated. "Maybe she needs to be alone. To calm down. She's probably just overtired." She turned to Paige, who didn't have the slightest idea why Katie was so upset. It couldn't have been the mention of driving again, could it? That certainly wouldn't send someone into hysterics. Would it? "I'll do your exercises with you tonight," her stepmother said. "In the playroom. That will give Katie some time alone. I think that's all she needs."

Bill shook his head in disapproval, but he said nothing.

"I disagree," Tuck said suddenly. "I think being alone is the last thing in the world Katie needs right now." Looking directly at Paige, he added, "You probably don't know this, but you weren't the only one hurt in that accident." Then without another word, he excused himself, collected his and Katie's dishes, and left the room.

Paige, a puzzled expression on her face, turned toward her parents. "Is Katie sick?"

"Oh, no!" Virginia Mae answered. "I don't have any idea what Tuck was referring to." She frowned. "And don't you start worrying about Katie now, Paige, you have enough on your mind."

"I know this much," Bill said. "Katie's been overloaded lately. Paige, you're getting around pretty well now. I think it's time to ease up on demanding help from Katie."

Paige had been thinking exactly the same thing. Katie didn't look too good. I'm the one who was hurt, she thought, but I've been able to keep my schoolwork and my newspaper work under control, thanks to Katie. I don't think she's in control of anything right now.

"Sure, Dad," she said aloud. "No problem." And she meant it.

But her good intentions lasted only until the following day. The exercises she had done with Virginia Mae had drained her. When she asked Katie to please get her some lemonade, she told herself it was because she couldn't have negotiated the stairs just then if her life had depended upon it.

Katie, lying face down on her bed, didn't answer. She had flung herself across the bed the minute she got home from swim practice and hadn't moved a muscle since then.

"Katie! Didn't you hear me? Could you please get me something to drink?"

Katie awoke reluctantly. "What?" Rubbing her eyes, she tried to sit up. But her body seemed to weigh a ton. "What did you say?"

"I need something to drink. I'd get it myself, but I'm really beat."

"Well, I'm beat, too." Katie swallowed the guilt that assailed her in refusing Paige's request. But it wouldn't kill her to get her own drink, would it? Hearing footsteps on the stairs, she called out, "Tuck?" Let him run Paige's little errand. It wouldn't kill him, either. But there was no answer from the hallway.

"Katie, you know better than anyone else what those exercises are like. You can't possibly be that tired. All I want is a little glass of something cold and wet."

Katie buried her head under the pillow. "Call Megan or Mary Emily," she said in a muffled voice. "They'll get it for you." Give it up, Paige, she thought wearily. Go get the stupid drink yourself.

"But you're here and they're not. Why can't you get it?"

There was no answer.

In her thirst, Paige had completely forgotten her father. "Katie, I can't believe you're ignoring me like this. How can you be so selfish? If it weren't for you — "

Katie sat bolt upright in bed, her mouth open in horror.

And just then Ben walked in. His expression was one of disgust. But it was directed toward Paige, not Katie.

"And I can't believe what you almost said," he said, his voice chilly. "You told me yourself the accident wasn't Katie's fault. And she's *not* your personal slave, Paige."

Sensing what was coming, Katie hauled herself out of bed and escaped the room.

When the door had closed behind her, Paige pulled herself up in bed. She was painfully aware of a Coke stain on her blue robe and a total lack of makeup on her face. "You don't understand," she began lamely, but he didn't let her finish.

"No, *you're* the one who doesn't understand. If you weren't so wrapped up in yourself, you'd see how hard all of this has been on Katie. I'm worried about her. Everyone is. Except you."

"That's not true! I know she's tired. Getting me a drink was the only thing I asked her to do for me today. And she wouldn't even do that one little thing."

"That one little thing and a thousand others," he said sarcastically. "You never let up on her, do you?"

That struck Paige as being totally unfair. She *had* taken it easy on Katie. And why hadn't he knocked before he'd come into the room? Barging right in like that was really rude.

"You're acting like a spoiled brat," Ben said. "It isn't your sister's job to wait on you."

"And you're being an insensitive clod!" Paige shouted, really angry now. "And she's not my — "

"I know, I know." Ben shook his head. "She's not your sister." And he turned and walked out of the room, disgust written in every step he took. He would have slammed the door if Jake hadn't appeared in the doorway just then. He didn't reply to Jake's casual, "Hi, Ben." Paige watched in disbelief as Ben disappeared.

Katie, exiting the bathroom, witnessed Ben's departure and Jake's arrival. Had Jake come to see her or Paige? She never knew these days. Well, there wasn't any law preventing Katie from talking to him, was there? After all, this was her house, too. And her bedroom. Why not confront him now, ask him exactly what was going on, why he had no time for her?

She reached the slightly opened door and stopped. Because she didn't like what she was hearing.

". . . and then," Paige was saying, "he practically accused me of browbeating Katie. And all I asked for was a drink!"

She's whining, Katie thought with contempt. I wonder if she knows she's whining.

Katie held her breath, hoping Jake would defend Ben. But her heart turned over as she heard

149

Jake say in a comforting voice, "Hey, take it easy, Paige. What does Ben know about being stuck in a bed for weeks at a time? He's a nice guy, but he never struck me as the type who was overloaded with compassion." Katie could almost hear Jake's shrug. "Forget it. I'm here. I'll get you a drink. What'll it be, Coke or lemonade?"

Terrified that he would discover that she'd been eavesdropping, Katie flew down the stairs. Grabbing a jacket, she left the house and ran down the street to the park.

The first bench she came to was occupied by a disconsolate Ben Collins. Not waiting for an invitation, she sank down beside him. He barely glanced up when she joined him. They sat in silence for several minutes, looking out over the park's almost-leafless trees, children playing on the sliding board and swings, women pushing strollers.

"I guess you think I'm pretty selfish," she said slowly. "I mean, all she wanted was a drink."

"And a thousand and one other things," Ben said harshly. "You're not selfish. She's been ordering you around ever since the accident. You shouldn't let her get away with it, Katie. You're not doing her any favors by waiting on her. She gets around pretty well on crutches now, and your dad told me she needs the exercise."

Her anger dissipated at Ben's understanding words. "Yes, but you've never seen what she goes through during her therapy." She shuddered. "It's rough."

"No excuses." Ben brushed a stray lock of straight brown hair away from his forehead.

"Don't make excuses for her. I'm sorry that she has to go through this. I hate it almost as much as she does. But pushing people around isn't going to change what's happened to her."

That kind of understanding was exactly what Katie had been hungering for for weeks. Tears of relief streamed down her cheeks, and she couldn't speak.

When Ben glanced over at her, he was shocked. "I didn't mean to make you cry. What did I say? I'm sorry!" He slid over closer to her and put an arm around her shoulders. "Hey, Katie, it's okay, really."

And Katie, so thankful to be comforted at last, thought how ironic it was: Here she was, in the park with Ben, while Paige and Jake were together at the house. The accident had done more than hurt a couple of people. It had turned their world upside down. Topsy-turvy, as Miss Aggie would say.

And right now, it looked very much as if it might stay that way.

Back at the house, Paige was thinking exactly the same thing. Jake had gone downstairs to get her drink, and the room suddenly seemed very empty. I shouldn't have implied that the accident was Katie's fault, she scolded herself. I know that it wasn't. And I know *she* thinks it was. The look on her face when I started to say that it was, was awful.

Paige shrugged and slid down under the covers. Did being sick make everyone this rotten? She knew everyone was sick to death of taking care of her. Everyone in the house, plus her friends, probably wished even more than she did that she'd get out of this bed and act like a human being again. If she didn't become more mobile pretty soon, they'd probably push her out of bed.

I'm trying, she thought angrily, *I am* trying. She hated the therapy, but she did it, anyway. Didn't that prove that she wanted to be completely healed?

Ben had been unfair. Okay, she had zapped Katie and she shouldn't have, especially after her father had asked her to take it easy. But Ben was supposed to care about her. She had a right to expect support from him, didn't she? And here was Jake, waiting on her and being understanding, and where was Ben? He was absent, that's where he was!

It wasn't just her physical health that was all wrong. It was everything!

Crazy, crazy world, she thought crankily as Jake arrived and handed her a glass of juice. Crazy. But it didn't keep her from smiling at Jake, and thanking him — the way she'd never thanked Katie.

CHAPTER 16

A cold front attacked Philadelphia later that week, bringing with it a driving rain and a blustery, cold wind.

Paige didn't care. Although she had been working very hard at becoming more and more mobile and could actually feel the muscles in the injured leg growing stronger, she still felt very much the prisoner. What difference did bad weather make to an invalid? Besides, she thought wickedly as she jump-hopped down the stairs with the aid of her yellow crutches, maybe this rotten weather will make Connie Tyler's party tonight a disaster. She couldn't go, and the frustration of constantly being left out of things filled her with ill will toward the whole world.

That was the mood she was in when Katie found her sitting alone in the living room.

"Mom called," Katie said cooly. She couldn't forget that Paige had cried on Jake's shoulders.

"She and Dad are staying in town for dinner. If the weather clears up, they'll be home later."

Katie sat down in her stepfather's recliner. She sighed, remembering Virginia's anxious, "Is Paige okay?" Katie had answered curtly, "Yes, she's fine." And then, after a moment, "And I am, too, although you didn't ask." She'd told her mother she'd see her later and hung up.

"And Tuck," she told Paige, "took Miss Aggie home. He didn't want her walking to the bus stop in this mess. And then he's taking Megan and Mary Emily out for hamburgers, since we're not having a family meal tonight."

Paige sent a gloomy look her way. "And I suppose you're off to Connie's party."

Katie knew all about Connie's party. It was a sixteenth-birthday celebration. She wasn't going because Connie's older brother Tim was a friend of Jake's. So Jake just might be there. And she didn't want to see Jake.

"I'm not going." Actually, sh*e did* want to see Jake. But not at a party. Not surrounded by dozens of people. Besides, Virginia Mae had made her promise that she would stay with Paige. "If I know someone is with her, I'll feel better," she had said.

Yeah, but will *I*? Katie wondered sullenly. Paige seemed to be suffering from an attack of bad attitude. The last thing in the world I need right now, Katie thought, staring at the floor, is her foul mood. I've already got one of my own!

"You don't have to baby-sit me," Paige said sourly. "Even if Virginia Mae made you prom-

154

ise." This was what she hated about her position more than anything else, this feeling in the family that she somehow needed to be watched all the time. "I'm not a heart patient who could go into cardiac arrest at any moment. I just have a bad leg, that's all."

Katie said nothing. Virginia Mae had given the order, and that was that. Even if she wanted to go to the party, she wouldn't dare. If anything could make her relationship with her mother worse than it already was, it would be leaving Paige alone in the house that night.

Paige lifted one yellow crutch and waved it in the air. "What can possibly happen to a person on crutches? It's not as if I can take off for parts unknown. I can't go explore the big, wide world out there." Her tone of voice grew harsh. "You need two good legs for that."

Rain slapped against the windows as a wave of sympathy washed over Katie Summer. Jake had accused her of not understanding what being an invalid did to someone as active and healthy as Paige. Maybe he was right. Being stuck in the house while everyone else around you was living a normal life must be really weird.

"You'll be able to go to parties pretty soon," Katie offered lamely.

Paige threw her a look of disgust. "I wanted to go to *this* one!" she shouted angrily, lashing out with one foot to give the footstool in front of her a healthy kick.

She screamed. In her anger, she had made the mistake of kicking with the wrong leg. The wounded leg. A shaft of pain shot up her leg from ankle to hipbone. It pushed her upright on the couch, clutching at the bandages.

"Oh, Paige!" Katie cried, jumping up. "What did you *do*?"

Rocking back and forth on the couch, Paige moaned and held onto the aching limb.

Frightened, Katie stood over her, feeling helpless. Why wasn't her mother home? She would know what to do. "I'll call the hotel," she volunteered over Paige's moaning. "Maybe Mom and Dad can come straight home."

Paige shook her head, gasping in pain. "No. No time. I have to get to the hospital. I think I've done something terrible to this leg. You'll have to take me there."

Katie's mouth dropped open. "Are you crazy? I can't. How can I?"

Paige looked up, her face a twisted gray mask. "Of course you can. The sedan's out front. You know it's been repaired. Mom rode in with Dad this morning and Tuck always takes her car. That leaves the sedan, right?"

"I didn't mean there wasn't a car here. I meant *I* can't drive it. Don't ask me, Paige. Please!"

"I *have* to ask you." Paige could barely speak, the pain in her leg was so intense. "You're all I've got. Now stop being so silly and go get your permit. I know you hid it. But you need it now, Katie. I'm a licensed driver, so you'll be perfectly legal, if that's what you're worried about."

"Paige, the weather is so bad out there, Mom and Dad didn't even want to drive home and

156

Dad's been driving for years." She was wringing her hands in distress. "What on earth makes you think I could do something he didn't think he could do? The streets are probably flooded!"

"Tuck went out. *He* wasn't afraid."

Katie brightened. "That's right! Let me see if I can catch him at Miss Aggie's. Maybe he's still there. He can come home and drive you to the hospital." She moved toward the telephone.

"KATIE SUMMER!"

Katie stopped in her tracks. "Katie, I am *not* waiting for Tuck!" Paige threw her head back and wailed, "I c-can't! I just can't!"

And Katie understood that she had no choice. She ran upstairs and dug her permit out of the bottom dresser drawer. Her hands were shaking, and she was praying fervently that Tuck would walk in through the front door before she had to walk out of it and get behind the wheel of that car.

Her prayers went unanswered. And her hope that by the time she got back downstairs, Paige would be fully recovered, evaporated the moment she saw Paige's pain-lined face.

I just have no choice, Katie thought, despair filling her. I have to take her to the hospital. I have to drive.

Maybe this was her punishment for causing Paige's injury in the first place.

Swallowing her terror, she grabbed raincoats for herself and her stepsister, the car keys, and her purse. Then she gently helped Paige off the couch, into the hall, and out the front door. It was pitch-black outside and still pouring. The lawn, sodden now, seemed to be covered with a

157

thin layer of plastic wrap, making the grass slippery. Katie held her breath as she supported Paige across the muddy mess to the car.

They made it without falling. Katie got Paige settled into the front seat and hurried around to the driver's side. Her feet, hands, and hair were soaked in seconds.

The windshield was covered with a solid curtain of rain, impossible to see through. She was shaking with fear as she turned the ignition key. In her nervousness, she applied too much pressure to the accelerator, as she backed down the steep driveway. They skidded sideways, the tires on Paige's side slamming into the curb.

"I'm sorry, I'm sorry, I'm sorry," Katie shrieked. "Oh, God, I can't do this!"

"Yes, you *can*!" Paige managed through pain-clenched teeth. "You have to! Now *go*!" Katie was a total nervous wreck. She'd probably get them both killed. If only Tuck hadn't picked tonight to treat Megan and Mary Emily to hamburgers.

But it wasn't Tuck Paige was angry with. It was herself. Kicking at a stool with her injured leg! Of all the dumb, stupid stunts!

Katie couldn't stop shaking. The wind howled around the car, taunting her. It seemed to be crying, "You ca-an't dri-ive! You ca-an't dri-ive!" It was almost impossible to see through the heavy rain draping the windshield. She could remember absolutely nothing of what she'd learned about driving and could only cling to the steering wheel in desperation.

"Katie, stop shaking!" Paige begged. "You're making the car jerk, and it's killing me."

Their stop-start movements had propelled them to the bottom of the hill. Katie steered the car over to the curb, sloshing it through deep puddles, and came to a complete stop.

"I can't do this, Paige," she said, her voice shaking. "We'll have to take a cab. I'll run back to the house and call one. You wait here."

But before she could move, Paige grabbed her arm. "Katie Summer Guthrie," she shouted, "you are not setting one foot outside of this car! I am *not* waiting for some stupid taxi when there is a perfectly capable driver sitting right beside me. Now turn that ignition key, step on the gas and GET. ME. TO. A. HOSPITAL. RIGHT. NOW!" Paige sank back against the seat, exhausted.

Katie stared at her. "What did you just say? About a perfectly capable driver? You can't mean *me*."

"Well, I certainly didn't mean me. It's taking every ounce of strength I have just to sit here, never mind driving. The only thing I'm capable of right now is screaming, which is exactly what I'm going to do if you don't start the car."

The wind rattled the car windows. Katie ignored it. "How can you trust me to drive you after what happened? And in case you've forgotten, it was raining that day, too."

Paige lifted her head. "I never blamed you for the accident. I told you it wasn't your fault."

"That's what you said at first. But then, when

Mom blamed me, you acted like you did, too. And I knew what you were about to say the other day when Ben walked in."

"Well, I was wrong. I meant to tell you later, but I forgot. I was just mad because you were bouncing around all over the place, and I was stuck in that stupid bed."

Katie made a rude sound. "I don't bounce anymore. I haven't bounced in a long time."

Ignoring that, Paige continued, "And Mom doesn't blame you."

Another rude sound.

"She doesn't blame you, Katie. She just feels guilty because it was one of his kids that got hurt the worst."

"His kids?"

"Yeah. My dad's."

"You mean she would have been happier if I'd ended up in the hospital?"

"Of course not. She didn't want either one of us hurt, silly. Will you *please* start the car? I think I'm going to faint."

Caught up in the conversation about Virginia Mae, Katie started the car, her motions automatic.

"I just meant," Paige continued, "that sometimes when you have two families mixed together, like ours, the parents take it personally when one of their kids is responsible for something that happens to the other person's kids."

Katie hadn't even noticed that she'd stopped shaking. "You mean like if I didn't clean our room, she'd get a lot madder than when you don't clean the room?"

"Ouch!" Paige said, but Katie could tell she was grinning. "Yeah, it's sort of like that." She was thinking of the all too frequent lectures from her father since Katie's arrival. "They both want us to be on our best behavior so the other parent won't disapprove of us. Because if they disapprove of the stepkid, they're saying we weren't raised properly *before* the marriage. Get it? They take it personally because to them it means that one or the other parent didn't do a good job."

Paige sounded like she knew what she was talking about. And sh*e was* older. Maybe she understood adults. Katie turned a corner slowly, to avoid skidding in the shallow rivers of water that filled the street. "It still sounds like she thinks I did something wrong."

Paige shook her head. "She doesn't. You talk to her when we get home, if she's there. If she isn't, call her up and ask her. You'll see that I'm right. She'll tell you."

Katie decided she would do exactly that the first chance she got.

"The guy ran a red light, Katie. It was *his* fault. You're a perfectly good driver. I was going to tell you that just before the creep slammed into us." That wasn't true, but Paige considered it a necessary little white lie.

"You were?"

"Yes, I was. And can you go a little faster, please? I'm dying here."

"You're not dying. And I can't go any faster," spoken primly, "because weather conditions won't permit it. Just relax, okay? We'll get there."

And they did. Katie, helping Paige from the car

161

at the emergency room entrance, felt a great sense of satisfaction. Conquering a terrible fear, she decided, was the greatest feeling in the world. She gave the sedan a fond pat as she left it and barely felt the pelting rain or the tugging wind as she helped Paige out of the car.

Paige hadn't broken anything. The only lasting injury was the blow to her pride when the young doctor in emergency said with a smile, "When one has a mangled leg, it is not wise to kick at anything more solid than whipped cream." He assured her the pain was only temporary and sent them on their way.

"I'll drive!" Katie said cheerfully as they went back out into the cold, wet darkness.

Paige, relieved that she hadn't done any permanent damage to her leg, hooted. "No kidding! Gee, I was kind of thinking I'd give it a shot!"

Katie laughed and got behind the wheel.

CHAPTER 17

The weather had improved a bit. The rain had tapered off to a steady drip, the wind settled down to an occasional gust. Comfortable behind the wheel, Katie suggested stopping for something to eat. "I'm starving to death! Everyone else in the family ate out tonight, why not us?"

"Oh, no," Paige countered, "I don't want to be seen in public like this. I'm a mess!"

Katie glanced over at her. "No, you're not. I like your hair piled on top of your head like that. It's cute. And it's not like you're in your pajamas. You're wearing perfectly respectable clothes. Come on, it'll do you good to get out."

Paige remained doubtful, but the unexpected compliment from Katie had thrown her off-balance, so she agreed to stop for food.

"My first outing," she murmured as they pulled up in front of a popular Italian restaurant. "I'd planned to spend hours getting ready for it, and here I am, wearing old jeans and a sweatshirt."

"Doesn't matter," Katie said, carefully parking the car. "Almost everyone is probably at Connie's party. And the ones that aren't will be so glad to see you out and about, they won't care if you've got a zillion zits."

Paige's hands flew to her face.

They both laughed.

"Of course," Katie added, "there may not be anyone here who's the least bit interested in us. In which case, at least we'll get fed. My stomach feels totally hollow. Let's go."

Being very careful with her injured leg, Paige got out of the car.

And, a few minutes later, was very glad she had. Because the first two people she noticed as she eagerly scanned the crowd, were Ben and Jake, seated in a booth by a window.

"Look who's here," she whispered to Katie. "Over there, by the window."

Katie looked, and her cheeks deepened in color. Jake looked super in a leather bomber jacket over a pale yellow sweater. And the smile he sent her made her knees weak. He signaled them, and before Katie could say, "No, I don't want to see him," Paige was tugging her toward the booth. Thinking that crutches didn't slow *some* people down at all, Katie followed. She was grateful that she was wearing her favorite pale blue turtleneck sweater and had brushed her hair in the hospital. If she was going to give Jake the cold shoulder, it would at least be a well-dressed cold shoulder.

It was awkward at first. They'd been through a strange, topsy-turvy period that had upset relationships and disrupted their day-to-day routines. Ben seemed uneasy to Katie, as if he weren't sure how to act around Paige now that she was back in the real world again. And Katie felt the same way as she sat down next to Jake. The last time she'd seen him, he'd been Paige's crying towel. And no one had even once tried to tell her that there was nothing going on between the two of them.

But Paige didn't seem the least bit interested in Jake now. All of her attention was focused on Ben, who was quickly relaxing in the face of Paige's high spirits. By the time their booth became encircled by a cluster of Paige's classmates wishing her well, Ben's hand held hers under the table.

"Busy tomorrow night?" Jake asked Katie softly, surprising her. "Look's like your sister's on the road to recovery. Time to get back to our own lives, right?"

He thought it would be that easy? She was glad to see him, glad to be sharing a booth with him, and happy that his hand had just closed over hers. But she had been hurting after the accident, too, and where had he been? He'd either been absent or with Paige, neither of which had done Katie any good at all.

Maybe if she just kept telling herself that Jake had simply wanted to help Paige and her family, because they'd been friends of his for a long time, she'd begin to understand. But couldn't he have helped both of them? Couldn't he have found just a little time for her, even though she wasn't flat on her back in a hospital bed? It seemed to her that if he really cared, he could have done just that.

But she was tired of feeling so alone. Whatever had gone wrong these past few weeks between her and Jake, they couldn't fix it by ignoring each other. If she wanted it fixed, she would have to talk to him about it. And she had never been the sort of person to hold a grudge.

"I'll check when I get home," she said lightly. "There might be something I have to do tomorrow night."

He grinned at her.

"But maybe not," she added quickly. "Call me tomorrow, okay?"

Turning her befuddled attention to Paige, she thought, Why, my goodness, she's being positively charming. I never knew she had it in her. Watching her stepsister smile and toss her head as she answered questions about the accident, Katie thought, Why can't she be like that at home? It could make all the difference.

Paige wasn't making a conscious effort to be charming. It was just so wonderful to be back among the living, to feel like she mattered. To feel that, even with her crutches, she was just like everyone else. She found herself wondering if all invalids felt the way she had — so isolated and . . . abnormal. She hoped they didn't. It was *not* a nice feeling.

Katie was amused, watching Paige give a melodramatic account of the car crash.

"And all of a sudden there was this *gigantic* truck . . ."

Was this the same Paige who, just a short time ago, had kicked a footstool while in the throes of a temper tantrum? That kick, she decided, had served two purposes. It had turned Paige into a human being again (with all the imperfections of any human being and then some, Katie thought dryly). And it had put Katie Summer Guthrie behind the wheel of a car again. That one little kick had accomplished all of that. Amazing! Sometimes all it took was a good kick. . . .

Now, she thought as she drank her Coke and smiled at Jake, now things *can* return to normal.

Whatever normal meant in the Whitman-Guthrie household.

How can Katie stop her stepsister before Paige does something she regrets? Read Stepsisters #7 RECKLESS SISTER.

CHEERLEADERS®

Don't miss any exciting adventures of the popular Cheerleaders of Tarenton High!

True love!   Crushes!   Breakups!   Makeups!

Read about the excitement—and heartache—of being part of a *couple!*

Order these titles today!

- ☐ 33390-9 #1 **CHANGE OF HEARTS** Linda A. Cooney
- ☐ 33391-7 #2 **FIRE AND ICE** Linda A. Cooney
- ☐ 33392-5 #3 **ALONE TOGETHER** Linda A. Cooney
- ☐ 33393-3 #4 **MADE FOR EACH OTHER** M.E. Cooper
- ☐ 33394-1 #5 **MOVING TOO FAST** M.E. Cooper
- ☐ 33395-X #6 **CRAZY LOVE** M.E. Cooper
- ☐ 40238-2 #15 **COMING ON STRONG** M.E. Cooper
- ☐ 40239-0 #16 **SWEETHEARTS** M.E. Cooper
- ☐ 40240-4 #17 **DANCE WITH ME** M.E. Cooper
- ☐ 40422-9 #18 **KISS AND RUN** M.E. Cooper
- ☐ 40424-5 #19 **SHOW SOME EMOTION** M.E. Cooper
- ☐ 40425-3 #20 **NO CONTEST** M.E. Cooper
- ☐ 40426-1 #21 **TEACHER'S PET** M.E. Cooper
- ☐ 40427-X #22 **SLOW DANCING** M.E. Cooper
- ☐ 40792-9 #23 **BYE BYE LOVE** M.E. Cooper
- ☐ 40794-5 #24 **SOMETHING NEW** M.E. Cooper
- ☐ 40795-3 #25 **LOVE EXCHANGE** M.E. Cooper
- ☐ 40796-1 #26 **HEAD OVER HEELS** M.E. Cooper
- ☐ 40797-X #27 **SWEET AND SOUR** M.E. Cooper
- ☐ 41262-0 #28 **LOVESTRUCK** M.E. Cooper

Complete series available wherever you buy books. $2.50 each